THE LAST NORTHWOODS READER

Copyright 1984
by Cully Gage
and
Avery Color Studios
AuTrain, Michigan 49806

Written by Cully Gage
Illustrated by Susan Van Riper Krill
Cover Photo by Hoyt Avery

Library of Congress Card No. 84-71820
ISBN 0-932212-38-7
First Edition - July 1984
Reprinted - August 1985
Published by Avery Color Studios
AuTrain, Michigan 49806

CONTENTS

If the language is sometimes salty and earthy, it was the usage of the time. We weren't very civilized in Tioga but we enjoyed our struggle for survival because we had a keen appreciation of the absurd. If you find memories and laughter in these pages, let me know.

Cully Gage

FOREWORD

"Tell me a story. Tell me another story," I'd beg my beloved Grandpa Gage when it was nearing bedtime. Now I'm hearing that myself not only from my own grandchildren but from others who have written me saying that they have enjoyed the first three Northwoods Readers and want one more.

"Mr. McGillicuddy," my grandfather would roar. "You ask too much too often of Sam, Sam, the pianner playing man. "However...." And then he'd tell me one more tale or two or three or more before concluding that it was time for both of us to go to bed.

I think this is my last Northwoods Reader. It's almost my bedtime.

Cully Gage

GALOOOM

Today Tioga is just a quiet little forest village in the heart of Michigan's Upper Peninsula but in the early years of this century when I was a boy it certainly wasn't very quiet. Before the iron mines closed we could hear the constant roar of the ore crusher going day and night, punctuated only by dynamite blasts and the clanking of ore cars. When the mine did shut down, the noise pollution didn't cease; we just heard all the other sounds that the mine noises had masked.

We noticed them mainly at night because often it was hard to get a good night's sleep with dogs barking, owls hooting, cats screaming at each other on our roofs, bullfrogs mating in the swamp east of Sliding Rock, trains whistling in the valley, and especially the horses and cows clomping up and down our pine board sidewalks. I don't know why they didn't walk on the road; perhaps they liked the sound of their hooves on the boards more than we did.

Our horses and cows roamed freely back then. All over town they ambled day and night munching. That is why every house had its own fence, picket or otherwise, to protect the family gardens that helped us make it through the winter. "Did you shut the gate?" was the commonest question heard by children. We not only had to shut the gate but be sure it was tightly latched because those horses and cows felt every fence was a challenge to be accepted. When thwarted, the horses whinnied, and the cows bellowed and rattled their cowbells. I've read poets who described the "lowing of cows in the green pastures." Our cows didn't low; they bellered. Hearing one shatter the night under your bedroom window with a terribly loud "Moooooooha-ah-ha" could sure jump you out of bed.

"Cully! Get that damned cow out of here before she eats the turnips," my father would yell. "You probably left that gate open again." I probably hadn't but no one ever argued with a father clad only in a long nightshirt. So out into the night I'd go, barefoot, with only my pants, on to do my duty. Now cows are ignorant bull-headed devils in the daytime when you try to drive them but at night in a turnip patch their obstinacy is enough to make you run out of cuss words and weep. And how they bellow in protest when finally you get them out of the gate. One night two other cows came in before I got the first one out and by the time I was able to crawl back in bed the roosters were greeting the grey dawn, crowing from every chicken yard in town, and then the dogs started barking. No Tioga was not a quiet little village in the forest.

I'd have to say that the dogs contributed most to the welter of sounds in which we were bathed. Others may argue the point but I would bet Tioga had more dogs than any town in the U.P., certainly more dogs than people. There were big dogs, little dogs, brown and black and gray dogs of every variety but that there was some hound ancestry in each was demonstrated every time we had a full moon. As it came up over the eastern hills, the mournful hound symphony would start at the very top of our hill street where the moonbeams first touched that hidden trigger in the guts of every hound or part hound dog that makes them howl. Then the baying would proceed in stages down the hill until all the French dogs down in the valley had joined the chorus. I used to lie there in bed wondering what they were trying to tell the moon with their long, lorn howlings. Perhaps they were aching for their lost wolf heritage I thought as I pulled the covers over my head.

Usually, and mercifully, there was a period after midnight when the howling stopped but at sun-up a new dog chorus began. This time it was not moon-howling but barking and it lasted until the dogs were fed or let out of the yards to forage the garbage heaps for themselves. Some barking and yapping continued all day long. One nasty little mutt three doors down from our house yapped four times every three minutes for fifteen years. After a time you got so you could ignore it unless by chance it only yapped three times. Then you started listening again.

Of all the dogs in town the one I liked to watch or listen to most was Pullo. First of all he was the dumbest dog that ever lived, and the laziest. Always smelling faintly or powerfully of skunk, old Pullo, despite a hundred encounters, had never learned that a critter with an arched striped tail was not a companion to nuzzle. Nor had he ever been able to remember that a porcupine has quills. He was the hound I've told about before that my cat, Puuko-the-Knife, used to ride like a jockey down the street every morning to service the French cats down in the valley. No, old Pullo was a slow learner and a creature of habit, always taking the same route from house to house hoping for a handout, even if that route made its way along our picket fence where Puuko lay in wait.

I've said that Pullo was the laziest dog in town and he was. If a deer fly lit on his nose when, as usual, he was lying on the grass by our back door, his big brown sad eyes would revolve around to focus on it but his nose never twitched. Except when our tomcat rode him down the hill Pullo never ran or loped. Just ambled along, every so often uttering a deep "Galooom." All of us liked to hear that Galooom of Pullo's; there was a sort of dignity in it, the only dignity that Pullo possessed because he was as ungainly and ugly a hound as every dreamed about a rabbit. Not that he ever probably did. Too lazy. If he dreamed at all he probably dreamed of some ancient bleached bone in a garbage pile. No matter. Sleeping in the sun on our board sidewalks or in the middle of the road, we stepped around or drove around his lazy carcass as he watched dreamily with only one eye open.

You never found Pullo cavorting around with other dogs; he preferred people, especially those with a bone or something in their hand. Pullo never begged for food either. He'd just sit or lie there by your back door waiting for hours if need be until his Galooom and sad eyes brought him his daily crust or bone. Because we just couldn't resist the old scoundrel he probably ate better than most. At least you couldn't see his ribs but perhaps that was because he believed in the conservation of energy. What you did see were the blue-black spots that covered his grey hide. A crazy looking dog, people said. Perhaps in his "mixed stuff," the terms we used to indicate uncertain ancestry in man or beast, there had been some Dalmatian coach dog or spotted leopard. Anyway, old Pullo was unique.

If there can be two unique dogs in a single village, Lulubelle was the other one. She was Aunt Lizzie's pooch. No mixed stuff, she was a pure bred white Pekinese. Aunt Lizzie boarded summer visitors occasionally and that fall some people from Chicago had come on the train to see the fall colors carrying Lulubelle in a little red basket. Originally they had planned to stay two weeks but when it rained hard every day they left a note for Aunt Lizzie, when she was at church, saying they'd taken the train for the Copper Country and would pick up the Pekinese on their return. They never did come back which was not particularly surprising. Ten minutes of Aunt Lizzie were aplenty and six rainy days with her must have been murder.

Lulubelle brought a new life to Aunt Lizzie. Having buried three husbands (our people claimed they were the only men in Tioga who ever died happily), she needed something to love, someone who would listen. Childless, she lavished on the mutt all the affection she might have given to a real baby. She held it for hours on her lap; she brushed the hair out of its beady little eyes; she cooked kidney and liver for it. When Lulubelle rolled on a very dead sparrow, Aunt Lizzie shampooed her until the fluffiness returned and then sprinkled her with cologne. She also bathed the dog in a continuous flood of the most nauseating baby-talk imaginable. I won't let my fingers put it on paper. When she had Emil Olssen and Eino Tuomi build Lulubelle a tiny doghouse to her specifications a lot of people came to look and laugh when they saw that it had a hardwood floor and front porch. Next she'll be putting a doll bed inside, they said. Eino and Emil felt like fools working on that doghouse.

Silly as Lulubelle looked by nature, Aunt Lizzie soon had her looking even worse. She clipped and trimmed her to look like a French poodle with rosettes of white hair at the base of her tiny shaved legs, then did the same with her tail. That cooled off Lulubelle considerably so Aunt Lizzie sewed her a little red jacket and some red stockings to match. Lord what a sight!

The first time Aunt Lizzie walked Lulubelle down our street they sure got a lot of attention. Though most of it was unfavorable ("My God, Aunt Lizzie, wot the hell is that?"), she didn't mind at all. She was used to unfavorable attention. Kids came out of nowhere to see the strange creature mincing along on its little short feet. Although Aunt Lizzie was armed with an umbrella to repel any possible threat to her sweetie-pie, the dogs that showed up took one look and one sniff to make sure it wasn't a cat, then walked away disgustedly. The cologne, no doubt! That day Aunt Lizzie made only three house calls and for once had little gossip to share. All she could talk about was the little cuddles in her lap and when that little cuddles had an accident in that lap at Mrs. DeCaire's house, all Aunt Lizzie said was "Oh you naughty, naughty little baby!"

Returning up the hill, Aunt Lizzie and Lulubelle met old Mr. Bones coming down, pulling his little red wagon behind him, the one with the jugs under the burlap bag. Smilingly polite as usual, Mr. Bones doffed his hat and bowed, then saw Lulubelle in her little red jacket and stockings. He bent down to get a better look and, having had a nip or two, he fell on his face. Recovering, he sat there talking to himself. "Mr. Bones," he said. "Looks like yer getting them heebee-jeebees again and Charley, he's a-going put you in jail again. Head for home, Mr. Bones, head for home!" He did and the trainmen at the station didn't get their jugs that day.

After carefully stepping around Mr. Bones, Aunt Lizzie and Lulubelle made their way up the board sidewalk only to find another obstacle in their path. It was Pullo taking another of his daily constitutional naps. As they passed, Pullo opened one bleary brown eye, then did a double take. A red and white albino skunk? Smelled pretty powerful but with a difference. Rousing himself, Pullo got to his feet somehow and followed them.

Quite a procession it was. First Aunt Lizzie with an umbrella in one hand and the red leather leash in the other, then Lulubelle prancing daintily in all her finery, with silly little tail held high, and then, bring up the rear, the big spotted grey hound.

Was it love at first sight or hind sight? Pullo didn't hurry, nor did he do anything but sniff that white little tail, but it was clear that he was intrigued. "Scat!" said Aunt Lizzie waving the umbrella as she quickened her pace. Pullo didn't scat; he just followed sniffing the cologne or something. Finally Aunt Lizzie swept Lulubelle up into her arms, went into her house and shut the door. Pullo lay down by the steps, lifted his head and uttered a long galooom.

From that time on Pullo became Aunt Lizzie's shadow. If she went to the store, the old hound followed her even if she'd left Lulubelle at home. On her daily gossip rounds, he accompanied her, waiting patiently by the gate until she'd had her coffee and conversation. People began to say that Pullo had become smitten of the old widow herself, another bit of evidence that he was the stupidest dog in town. I don't believe it though because he was a different dog when Aunt Lizzie had Lulubelle on the leash or in her basket. Only then did he put back his head to bay; only then did he seem half awake.

It sure pestered Aunt Lizzie to have Pullo following her so constantly but nothing she did dissuaded him, not even being beaten by her umbrella one Sunday. Pullo had followed her to church of course and was lying there by the open door during the service nice and quiet until Aunt Lizzie sang a solo part in the choir. Now usually she could hit the lower notes fair and square but she sharped and flatted and wobbled and screeched the high ones so badly it was all the congregation could do to keep their fingers out of their ears. Well, when Pullo heard Aunt Lizzie yelping those high notes, he poked his head in the door and started accompanying her, not only with galooooms but other hound wails as well. We laughed so hard there wasn't a dry eye in the house, and the old hound never got so many hand outs as he did the week after the duet. Naturally, Aunt Lizzie was furious, and she whacked old Pullo so hard after the service that the preacher reproved her. Pullo followed her home.

The long winter came and passed and finally it was spring. Oh lovely U.P. springtime with its arbutus, cowslips, violets, adder's tongues - and every dog in town with the lust gleam in its eye. Aunt Lizzie knew that Lulubelle needed to get out of the house, needed grass to roll on, needed sun. She also knew that gleam so she hired Emil and Eino to build a three foot high chickenwire fence in her sideyard, complete with a gate, and the little doghouse within it. Pullo supervised.

Aunt Lizzie did her utmost to chase him away with a broom when she first put Lulubelle in the yard but he wouldn't go. All Pullo did was to move from the back steps to the fence. There he stretched out beside it, yawning in the sun. Not even when Lulubelle was placed inside the yard did he open more than one eye. Just his nose wrinkled. Aunt Lizzie kept a sharp watch for an hour or so but nothing happened even when Lulubelle went up to the fence between them and squeaked. Didn't really bark, or yap, or yip, or howl; all that poor excuse of a dog could do was squeak, but once Pullo answered back with his galooom. A platonic friendship, nothing more? Maybe the old hound's glands were as lazy as the rest of him.

None of the other dogs in town seemed particularly interested in Lulubelle either. Gangs of them were too busy chasing other females in heat. It was spring. The whole town rang with their barking as they swirled around up and down town, fighting, snarling, and mounting each other when they couldn't get near the she dog with the come-hither fragrance. When they passed by Pullo, the old dog didn't even twitch.

A bit later, spring came to Lulubelle too although Aunt Lizzie didn't know it at first. Out in her yard the Pekinese was very restless, strutting around with her silly little tail held high. She'd come to the fence where Pullo lay, squeak at him, then run back to her doghouse, then do it again. The old hound was apathetic, almost bored with her antics, but he kept a sad brown eye on her. Once they touched noses through the wire; once she backed up to the old hound's nose and wiggled her hind end seductively. That made him open the other eye but still he made no movement toward her. The laziest, stupidest dog in town.

This went on for about three days before the other dogs caught wind of Lulubelle. Then all hell broke loose. Dogs came from all over town, big ones, little ones, black ones, brown ones. They jumped and broke down Lulubelle's fence and tried to jump her. Terrified, she dived into her little doghouse, the door of which was too small to let them enter. Somehow the doghouse got turned upside down in the melee but, because of its hardwood floor, Lulubelle was still safe.

Out came Aunt Lizzie, flailing away at the dogs with her broom but there were just too many of them. People said they could hear the old gal yelling and the dogs barking as far as Flinn's store. Aunt Lizzie finally snatched up the doghouse with Lulubelle in it but didn't make it to the back door before one big hound mounted her leg. And where was Pullo during all this excitement? Lying calmly beside the fence with only one eye open.

Aunt Lizzie was certain that she had rescued Lulubelle in the nick of time and that her maidenhood or head was intact but some months later it became apparent that she was wrong. Lulubelle gave birth to three hound pups that later on developed blue-black spots just like Pullo's. And when they got big enough to howl, they laid back their heads and bayed "Galooom!"

How had that stupid, lazy old bugger done it?

Probably on his knees.

Galooom!

GRANDMA NEEDLES THE PREACHER

When I was a boy I had two grandmothers who lived in our home at different times. I think I've already told you about Grandma Gage, that old she-devil, who was so mean to the grandpa I loved so dearly. For years and years she had bossed and humiliated him until finally he rebelled and dewigged her at our dining table. My Grandma Van, in sharp contrast, was the sweetest little old lady you could find anywhere. Her face, despite its eighty nine years, was always serene and almost without wrinkles. Smiling and chuckling to herself as she relived some ancient memory, it was good just to be around her. Besides, when I'd been up to some devilment and had been banished to my upstairs bedroom, I'd sneak in to see Grandma Van for the love and comfort that was always there. She'd get out a tall glass bottle of striped candy sticks, give me one with a hug, then tell me a wonderful story about her early days.

16

With her father, two brothers, and her Aunt Patience, Grandma Van had come to southern Michigan by Erie canal boat and covered wagon in the late 1840's. At times Grandma Van was a bit foggy, (she always had trouble remembering where she'd put her Civil War pension check. It was always under her mattress) her memory of the early days was still very vivid.

Mother always knew where to find me on a rainy afternoon because I was always up with Grandma Van, listening. Sometimes she'd read me a bible story, for she seemed to read the bible constantly, but at other times she would reminisce and I liked that better. "Tell me about the old days, Grandma," I'd beg. I wish I could remember half her tales. One that she told several times was about the long trek west from New York State. Grandma had walked much of the way except for the week on the Erie Canal because the oxen that pulled the covered wagon ploddled so slowly. Getting lost when the old wagon ruts had petered out, the oxen and wagon had become mired in a swamp and they lost a day unloading the wagon and building a corduroy bridge out of logs to get them out. And she told of the time the men were out hunting and three Indians came to their campfire demanding food. Grandma and her Aunt Patience cooked them corn-cakes over the open fire, cooking them slowly and making them small to gain time until the men returned.

The days of the Civil War were as yesterday to Grandma. One of her brothers had been killed at the second battle of Bull Run; another was grievously wounded at Antietam. Her fiance, Lewis Van Luke, came back from the war a broken man but she married him and nursed him back to health. Grandma Van always got very angry at the "Johnny Rebs" when she talked about the war. "Mark my word, Cully," she'd say, her nose twitching, "They'll get their comeuppance once Grant takes Richmond." Grandma's nose always twitched when she was mad. Often, when I saw her nostrils fluttering, I'd ask her what she was thinking about. "Them copperheads!" she'd answer. "President Lincoln ought to shoot every one of them."

I knew that copperheads were poisonous snakes that lived in the south but until my mother explained that the term had also been used to refer to the northern sympathizers with the confederacy, I couldn't understand why Grandma Van's worst epithet for anything she hated was "Copperhead." Why, she even used it for the bats that occasionally came into the house to terrify her, or for the bears that climbed our apple trees. "Copperhead!" and "Drat!" were Grandma Van's two cuss words.

Although there were times when Grandma Van became a bit mixed up about what was present and what was past, most of the time she was very sharp. Daily she surprised us by quoting something from the Bible that was extremely pertinent, always citing the book, chapter and verse from which it came. When my father brought back a huge basket of trout he had caught Grandma intoned "Ah, the morning stars sang together and all of the sons of God shouted for joy. Job: 38, verse 2." When I fought with my little brother Joe, she shook her head reprovingly. "Behold how good and how pleasant is is for brethren to dwell together in unity. Psalms: 133, verse 1." Yes, Grandma Van sure knew her bible.

But I must tell you about Grandma and the preacher. Few of the ministers assigned to our little Methodist-Episcopal church in Tioga ever stayed very long. Certainly it was hardship duty. The two big potbellied stoves, even when fired up the night before, rarely warmed the church enough in winter to prevent all of us from wearing our coats through the service. Indeed, you could usually see the white breaths of the thirty or so faithful rising up from the hard pews to heaven. Some said the church fathers used our Tioga church as a testing ground for new ministers or as punishment for older ones who had caused trouble somewhere else. Anyway we got some doozies over the course of years.

Our new preacher, the Reverend J. Plummer Jones, was evidently another of the odd balls. My mother came back from his first sermon almost in tears. "Oh, John," she said to my father. "He's a horrible man. Has a voice like a rasp and he said some terrible things about the Catholics and Lutherans. He's sure to cause trouble in Tioga."

"What did he say?" asked my father. Dad never went to church, having lost his faith in medical school. He said the first time he went to church they poured water over his head along with some Mumbo Jumbo; the second time they saddled him with a wife; and he expected that the third time they'd take him out, put him in a hole and throw dirt on his face. He wasn't exactly an athiest, he said, but an agnostic who worshipped all the gods and little fishes. Yet one of his best friends in town was Father Hassel, the gentle Catholic priest, with whom he played chess weekly as they sipped a glass of whiskey together and smoked one of the cigars our undertaker always sent each of them for Christmas. Both of them were good men caring deeply for their flocks.

My mother was trying to remember the new preacher's sermon. "For one thing, he told us that Catholics weren't true Christians, that they worshipped idols, that they prayed to statues and pictures of their saints, and that they had a false bible not like ours. He said their priests don't marry but only because some lewd Eye-talian pope in Rome says they can't. He said it was OK for them to have housekeepers though, and who knows what goes on in the confessional when a priest has a young girl sinner in it..."

Dad's laughter interrupted her. "I'll have to tell Father Hassel that," he said. "Mrs. Reilly is his housekeeper and she's not only old but the ugliest woman in the county. What did he say about the Finn Lutherans?"

Mother couldn't remember exactly. "I forget," she answered. "But it was most unpleasant. John, he's going to hurt our town if we don't get rid of him in a hurry. He'll get the old divisive prejudices heated up all over again."

My father nodded. "But what did he say about the members of his new flock? I'd bet he got in a little hell and damnation for our small small sins, didn't he?"

"Oh yes," mother replied. "We're all dirty sinners going to hell. 'Don't tell me you haven't had a dirty sinful thought since breakfast,' he roared. John, I'll admit I had several during the course of that sermon, it was so awful. And then he even had the nerve to demand a bigger salary. That in his first sermon! I don't know if I'll ever go to church again."

Grandma had been listening. "A copperhead!" she said. "Another copperhead! Run him out of town on a rail. 'How art thou fallen from heaven, O Lucifer! 'Isaiah 14: 12."

Our Methodists had a rough time during Reverend Jones' mercifully short stay with us. The Catholics and Finn Lutherans, yes, and the Holy Jumpers too, were mad at them. In vain we tried to disassociate ourselves from the preacher's attitudes and evil tongue but to no avail. That ancient weapon -ostracism - came into play. Finns and Catholics simply refused to talk to a Methodist. They wouldn't even respond to a greeting; just looked hard into your eyes and said nothing. Even their kids wouldn't play with me and they gave me some good beatings for no reason at all.

As the number of people going to our church plummeted, the Reverend Jones began to seek his sinners in their lairs. He came to our homes, often at the wrong times, and preached at anyone who opened the door. Moreover, he always came to the front door, not knowing that in our village it was used only for funerals and such.

For some reason, our own family had not been blessed by his visitation and my father speculated that it was because we were the only angels in town. But finally, the day came. Mother, always the lady, bade the minister welcome, ushered him into the living room where Grandma Van and I were sitting, and introduced us, then left to prepare afternoon tea and cakes. I remember that Grandma was darning holes in socks, using her ebony ball with the silver handle, and a good sized needle to hold the yarn. I'd been reading David Copperfield and tried to shrink into my corner as the preacher fixed me with a glare.

"Young man," he demanded. "Do you go to Sunday School?"

"Yes, sir."

"Have you learned anything? Who was Adam?" He sounded angry.

That was easy. "Adam was the first man that ever was invented," I replied. Of course I knew it anyway but the old Baptist Sunday

School song was running through my mind - you know the one whose chorus goes:

"Young folks, old folks, everybody come,
Join the Baptist Sunday School and have a lot of fun,
Ladies, check your chewing gum and raisins at the door,
And come and hear the Bible stories you've never heard before."

The verse about Adam was what made me use the word "invented."

"Adam was the first man that ever was invented.
He lived all alone and never was contented.
God made him out of mud in the days gone by,
And hung him on the fence for the sun to dry."

"And who was Noah?" The preacher scowled at me. That was easy too. I almost sang the verse:

"Along came Noah, stumbling in the dark,
Picks up a hammer and builds himself an ark,
In came the animals, two by two,
The hippokangaramus and the hippokangaroo."

But all I said was that Noah built the ark.

The Reverend Jones still wasn't satisfied. "Who were the three men who survived the fiery furnace?" There was a gleam in his eye. Thought he had me, I guess, but for some reason I knew the answer even though it wasn't in the song. "Shadrach, Meeshak and Abednego. Shadrack, Meeshak and Abednego," I chanted. I don't know why, but those three names had rung a gong in me when I'd first heard them. I'd sung them when skipping rope, or sawing firewood.

Over the glasses on the end of her nose, Grandma gave me a swift look of approval but said nothing. Then the preacher really got me. "Have you been baptized?" he asked. That was a sore point because I hadn't been and some of my Catholic playmates had told me I was sure going to Purgatory unless I had. When I asked my mother why not, she said my father had opposed it, saying that I should wait until I was old enough to make the choice myself. For that matter, I hadn't been circumcised either and the Finn kids with their skinned weiners told me I'd be sure to get the clap. All these thoughts were chasing each other inside my skull.

"What's the matter, young man? The cat got your tongue?" the preacher said impatiently. Grandma's nose began to twitch.

I told him I hadn't been baptized but probably would when I was old enough.

"Old enough?" he roared. "What do you mean, old enough? Do

you know, young man, that if you were to die tonight and haven't been baptized that you'd be in hell come morning?" That scared me. Maybe the French Canadian kids had been right. For some time I'd been worried every night when I said the prayer:

"Now I lay me down to sleep,
I pray the Lord my soul will keep
If I should die before I wake.
I bless the Lord for Jesus sake."

I was relieved when he turned to Grandma. "Madam," he demanded. "Are you saved?"

Grandma Van peered at him over her glasses. "Who are you?" she asked.

"I am the Reverend J. Plummer Jones, your pastor of the Methodist Episcopal church."

"Hallelujah!" said Grandma.

"I beg your pardon, ma'm. What did you say?"

"I said, 'Hallelujah." she replied evenly.

"And I asked you if you were saved." The preacher's voice sounded irritated.

Grandma looked up from her darning. "No, young man. After four score and nine hard years I'm not saved. I'm spent."

I almost giggled but the Reverend Jones had no sense of humor or didn't get the play on words. "Why haven't I seen you in church?" he demanded.

Grandma had good reason for not going to church. With a hip that hurt constantly, just going upstairs was a long and painful undertaking. Besides she had what she called "sky-atikky" (Sciatica).

" 'Though art a man of strife and a man of contention.' Jeremiah, 15:18', Grandma quoted. " 'Lord, lettest thy servant depart in peace.' Luke 2, 27.' " I could tell she was furious by the twitching of her nose.

He added to her fire. "Old woman," he said. "You know of course that you are a sinner in the eyes of the Lord?"

"Let him that is without blame cast the first stone!" Grandma was upset with herself because she'd forgotten the source. "Copperhead!" she muttered under her breath. "Copperhead!"

The Reverend J. Plummer Jones got down on his knees beside her and prayed for her rotten old soul. "Dear Lord," he intoned. "May this poor old woman come to see the evil of her ways and return to thy bosom. And also, Lord, may she, despite her dotage, come to have some respect for thy servant, J. Plummer Jones. Amen."

Well, that was too much even for Grandma. As he arose from his knees she took her darning needle and sank it to the hilt of his rump. Then came the howl of howls! The preacher bolted from the room, crashed into my mother bringing a tray of tea things and out of the front door he went. Before the door slammed shut however, I heard him shout something about getting the hell out of this Sodom and Gomora of a village.

He did, too. Within the week he was gone forever and Tioga gradually healed its wounds. "Hallelujah!" said Grandma. "A no count copperhead!"

U.P. POLITICS

The two men on the railroad section crew were resting after finishing laying the frog. A frog? Yes, that's what the heavy iron device is called that permits, at a switching point, the wheels and flanges of the wheels to cross over from one rail to another. The day before, Jules Fontaine and Matt Mattila, pumping the handcar on their patrol, had felt and heard something wrong as they passed over the switch by the Wabik siding. Investigating, they had discovered that one frog had sheared. A dangerous business, that; a train could be derailed. The two men had worked since dawnlight to fix it. Now they could take it easy.

Matt and Jules had been close friends for years, their lives paralleling each other like the tracks they tended. They'd been in the same grade throughout their schooling which had stopped after eighth grade because they had to help their families financially by cutting pulpwood for Silverthorne and Company. They had played basketball together on the town team, had married at about the same time, Matt a Finn girl and Jules a French Canadian. Jules had been the first one to get a job on the railroad section crew and, when an opening occurred, he made sure that Matt heard about the job before anyone else. They had hunted and fished as well as worked together for years.

Despite, or perhaps because of their close relationship, the Finn and the Frenchman were always competing with each other. Who could cut the most pulp or catch the most trout or make the most baskets? Who could lift the most railroad ties? First one man and then the other won the little battles for they were very evenly matched. In a booth at Higley's saloon for an hour each Saturday night they competed to see who could drink the most beer in five minutes or who could arm-wrestle the other down. Some evenings Jules won; other evenings Matt did. Always there was a lot of kidding but never any ill feeling. They were friends!

After they had sat silently on the platform of the handcar for some time, Jules suddenly said, "Hey Matt, how about a race?" The big Finn looked at him. "You crazy Frenchman, you're pooped and so am I. OK, how far?"

"No," replied Jules. "I got good mind to run for Township Treasurer next month. Why you no run too and we see who win?"

The enormity of the idea took some time to digest; yes, half a corncob pipe's smoking it took before Matt spoke. "What you and me know about treasuring?" he asked.

"Nothing. All I know it pays fair. Maybe one hundred bucks a year and ten dollar for meetings. Lots of beer money there, Matt."

"What you got to do for earn it?" asked the Finn.

"Me, I don't know. Collect tax moneys, I think. Put in bank." Jules grinned. "You scared I beat you, eh Matt?"

"No," said his partner. "I scared I win."

Politics had never been very important to the residents of Tioga. Oh, there'd been some real excitement when Teddy Roosevelt, the Rough Rider of the war with Spain, ran against Taft and Wilson by forming his Progressive, the Bull Moose party. We liked Teddy. He was a real man, a mighty hunter, an outdoorsman. Moreover, he was the only presidential candidate before or since to visit the U.P. while campaigning. Of course, some crazy fool shot and wounded Teddy at a speech in Negaunee, a shameful act that made us his devoted partisans. Besides, his people passed out little lapel buttons having the form of a bull moose. I traded a jack knife to get mine, and all of us felt let down when Woodrow Wilson won, that damned college professor and Quaker. Mostly, in the presidential elections, we voted Republican.

The township elections held little interest. For one thing, the same people had staffed all the positions for years and years. My father, Dr. Gage, had always been supervisor; Carl Johnson, the telegrapher down at the depot, had always been clerk; Charley

Olafson, the constable, and old Mr. Peterson, the treasurer. Rarely had any of them ever been challenged at the polls and the few times they had been they walloped the newcomer handily. While most of our people were registered and voted in the presidential elections because they were patriotic, only a handful of the most conscientious dropped their folded ballots through the slot in township elections.

But Mr. Peterson, the treasurer, had finally died, leaving his position wide open to all comers. The only persons who sought nominating petitions were Matt and Jules. Neither had trouble getting the necessary number of names but all those on Jules' petition were French names and all those on Matt's were Finnish. This should have warned them but they were sure surprised and upset when the campaign split the town in two, the Finns against the French, the Protestants against the Catholics. Home made posters began to dot the telephone posts: "Vote for Matt, not the Pope," "Don't let the Finns Run the Town, Vote for Jules!" Both men tried to scotch the rising tide of acrimony but failed, the old feelings of enmity just ran too deep. Father Hassel tried too, and so did the Finnish preacher, but to no avail. When a poster that read "Do You Want A Half Breed Frenchman to Collect Your Taxes?" Matt Mattila tore it down from the door of the town hall with his own hands and roamed the street with blood in his eye, trying to find the person who had put it there. When Pierre Dupont made an especially derogatory remark about Matt Mattila in his presence, Jules knocked him down. "Nevair there be so fine man as Matt Mittila," he said. "I going vote for him myself." All the turmoil had no effect on their friendship.

As election day approached, the two men became worried about what the job of treasurer required so they came to my father's house one evening to ask some questions. "Doctor," said Jules, "Looks like me or Matt going be treasurer. How much the job pay and what we got to do?"

Dad got down the Michigan Statutes book and began to read but soon Jules objected. "No, Doctor. Don't read that lawyer talk. Tell us."

"All right," said my father. "Your remuneration, I mean pay, would be fifty dollars a year, plus ten dollars for each board meeting, plus a percentage of your collection fees which must not exceed three hundred dollars. I as the supervisor get a hundred a year and an extra hundred for doing the tax roll. The clerk gets fifty and extra for meetings. Our constable as night watch gets eighty a month. So that's the pay, and I might say that as treasurer you'll earn every cent of it."

Jules and Matt looked apprehensive. "What we got to do, Doctor? What we got to do?"

"Well," Dad said, "Your main duties are to collect the tax money and write the checks to pay the township bills. You'll have to learn to keep books, of course, putting down each instance of income and outgo because they may be audited upon proper request."

"What that mean, Doctor?"

"It just means that some accountant from Marquette may look at your books if you've been crooked."

"We're honest," they assured my father.

"I know that and so does everyone else but you still have to have evidence of the fact. The main job, however, is to collect the taxes and deposit the money in the bank at Ishpeming as it comes in. That means you'll have to take a day off from work every so often to go there and get the business done." Dad didn't notice how their faces fell. When you worked for the railroad, you didn't ask for time off to do anything except to go to a funeral.

My father brought out the huge ledger that contained the tax roll. Opening it on the table before them, he patiently explained what it contained. "Here's the name of the property owner," he said. "And here's the description of this particular property. See, the SW¼ of the SE½ of Section 36, Town 49 North, Range 30 West. In your letter to the owner you must put that down exactly." Jules rolled his eyes!

"Now in this column we have the assessed valuation, in this instance $1372. That too has to go in your billing letter. Don't make a mistake in copying that assessment." Matt looked a little sick.

"Now here in column four we come to the actual tax," Dad continued. "I've got it all figured out for you by multiplying the assessed valuation of $1372 by the tax millage of 3.5 mils which gives us $48.02. That's the tax the owner must pay after you send him the bill." The two men slumped in their chairs.

"I might say," Dad added, "that you'll find some of our people mad at you when they get your letter because their taxes will be higher this year. You'll have to explain to each of them that in the election we held last June an extra half mil was approved so we could put a new roof on the school, install a new septic tank and perhaps build a new outhouse. It's only for one year but they'll give you hell, not me, because the tax letter will come from you." Dad grinned but Jules and Matt sure didn't. What had they gotten into?

"How many letters we got to send out?" one of them asked.

Dad ran his eyes up and down the pages of the ledger, counting. "Oh, I'd say maybe four hundred or more all told. And then you'll have to send out the same number again after they've paid so they can have their receipts. Be sure to make a copy of the first billing letter so all you have to do is write "PAID" and sign your name."

Eight hundred letters to write? Neither man had written more than four or five in his lifetime. Get the figures right; get the money to the bank; have people mad at you? Keep books? Matt and Jules were so overwhelmed they didn't hear my father saying, "And of course, you'll have to serve on the Board of Review to judge whether or not a taxpayer's protest is valid or not..."

"I quit!" said Matt. "Me too," said Jules. They put on their caps.

"Oh no, you don't! You can't quit now; the ballots are all printed with your names on them." Dad was exasperated. "You should have thought about the work a teasurer has to do before getting nominated. Now it's too late. Your only way out is to lose the election." Jules and Matt headed for the saloon. No arm wrestling this time. Silently, they drank and drank until Higley kicked them out and told them to go home.

The next morning, pumping the handcar on patrol, the atmosphere between the two men was strained for the first time in their lives. Finally Jules spoke. "Matt, I sorry I got you into this. I damn fool."

"I sorry too, Jules, but I damn fool too. We no politics men; we railroad men." Matt smiled a little for the first time since they'd talked with my father.

Although previously neither man had done any active campaigning at all, now they really beat the bushes. Each day in their own territory they tore down their own signs and put up new ones advocating the other. Every day after work Matt went around from house to house with the same message: "You my friend, Arvo?" "Yah, I you friend." "Then you vote for Jules. I no want job. I no can handle tax money." He campaigned for Jules at the sauna, in the saloon, even after church. When Matt saw John Niemi who owed him money for helping paint his house, he said, "You vote for Jules and I forget you owe me."

The French Canadian was doing the same. On the door of the blacksmith shop he placed a huge sign made from store wrapping paper "Don't vote for me. Vote for Matt. I don't want job. Jules Fontaine." You could see it all the way from the depot. He too went from house to house along with his wife Marie trying to explain why he was unfit for the job of treasurer, begging them earnestly to vote for his rival. He even split firewood for the Widow Gamaine and, refusing her thanks, asked her not to vote for him.

When election day finally arrived, Jules and Matt took the day off work to be outside the Town Hall when the voters lined up to cast their ballots. "Vote for Jules, not me!" "Vote for Matt. I'm going to. You do too." All their effort was in vain. Some people thought it was just friendship that made them talk that way. But the Finns all voted for Matt and the French Canadians for Jules and when the ballots were counted it was a tie. The election board workers, with Matt and Jules looking anxiously over their shoulders, counted them again. The result was the same: Matt Mattila 47; Jules Fontaine 47. Charley Olafson tossed the coin and Jules won - or lost - becoming thereby the new township treasurer. Matt didn't congratulate him; he just bought the beer at Higleys until the saloon closed that night.

The next day, Jules took the train for Ishpeming to see Clancy the lawyer and was overjoyed to find that yes, he could quit. The lawyer composed a formal letter of resignation and charged him ten dollars. Jules did not begrudge the money at all, and when he handed the letter to my father and was told it was legal and he was free, he could hardly keep from singing all the way down our hill street.

I suppose I should tell what happened after that. The township had to have a treasurer but nobody wanted the job. After two weeks my father went down to ask Ed Stenrud, our undertaker, if he'd fill in. "No," said Ed. "You know I've got heart trouble, Doctor. I don't need that worry too." But in the end, after pressure by both Dad and Father Hassel, the priest, he gave in. After all for business reasons, an undertaker has to keep on the good side of the doctor and the priest, and they made damned sure he knew it. So, in the end, we had a treasurer.

The only trouble was that before he could send out the year's tax bills, Ed Stenrud died.

THE WELL

eople have asked me what it was like to live in the little forest village of Tioga during the long winter time. What did we do? How did we pass the time when the winds blew cold and the snow drifts crept over the window sills? I've never been able to give a satisfactory answer. Certainly we were never bored even though, back there at the turn of the century, we had no radio or TV. Few of our families even got a newspaper. The Bible, the Old Farmer's Almanac, and the Sears Roebuck catalog provided our basic reading. The one thing we did have that helped us through the winter was talk.

For one thing, talking to each other helped us to bear the feeling of isolation that otherwise would have beset us. Back then a little village like ours was truly isolated. There were no automobiles, no roads, just wagon ruts through the forest. Only our railroads connected our little towns, so most of us just stayed put. Yet, by talking to each other and knowing everyone in town, and everything that happened to each of us, we managed to create the illusion that we were not lost and alone in the woods.

If Mrs. Sicotte burned a hole in her oven, the whole town knew about it before sundown, and someone had told her about someone who had an old range they weren't using. If the French Canadian girl, Colette Dubois, had been seen walking hand in hand with Toivo Upsalla down the railroad tracks, everyone knew that too. When Sulu shot that fourteen-point buck near the bridge over King's Creek, there were five men waiting to admire it when he dragged it home.

The talking took place everywhere - in the sauna, in the stores, at the post office, in the saloon and railway depot and, of course, in our homes. We did a lot of visiting back and forth during the winter, dropping in on neighbors for the cup of the coffee that was always on the stove, or, if the people were French Canadian, for croissants and a little glass of red wine. When two people met each other on the street they never just said hello or good morning. It was mandatory to spend a few moments in conversation before going on. If you didn't, it meant you were mad at each other.

Yes, we knew each other in Tioga. We knew all about each other's personal histories. When Unti Haitema was caught swiping a handful of dried apricots up at Flinn's store, everybody remembered that his grandfather had once sawn down half a forty of spruce that was on the mining company land adjacent to his own. Of course, that could have been a mistake in running the line, but we remembered. Generally speaking, most of the sins of Tioga were small, small sins, primarily because you just couldn't get away with anything without everyone in town knowing about it.

When something happened or someone did something we couldn't understand, we had a fine time speculating about the reasons behind it. For example, when Mrs. Sicotte burned that hole in her oven, was it because that stove was just too old? After all, it had been handed down to her by her Aunt Julie when the Sicotte's were first married. Or had they run short of good firewood and started burning dry tamarack poles from the swamp? Tamarack made too hot a fire. Or maybe she'd poured too much kerosene on the kindling in starting it? All speculation, of course, but it was talk stuff. Didn't much matter what we said to each other. So long as we were talking, we weren't alone in that wilderness. It wasn't just gossip; it was the sharing of our lives.

I had to explain all this so you could understand why we talked so often about Axel Erickson. He was a puzzlement and had been one during the twenty years or more that he'd lived in Tioga. Of course we had a few facts to go on. He'd come from Sweden in his early twenties, as his accent with the upward inflection at the end of his sentences still showed. At first he'd been a lumberjack for Silverthorne and Company, then later a hard rock man in our mine until he got caught in the big dynamite explosion in the Number Six stope. That was the cause of his difficulty in hearing. He was pretty deaf, Axel was. You had to almost shout in his left ear before he could understand. Then, ever since, he had been steadily employed as a section hand for the Duluth, South Shore and Atlantic. A fine worker, they said. Didn't soldier a bit even when the others of his crew were goofing off.

For example, once, on a terribly hot afternoon, when the other two men of the section crew, worn out from laying new ties in the heat, took a half hour swim in the pool below Red Bridge, Axel would not join them. Said he couldn't swim. That was all right but why did he have to keep on working by himself rather than sitting under a tree. The men kind of resented that.

Strong too for his size, Axel could man one of the bars of the hand-car when it took two to pump the other bar when they were coming back up the grade from Clowry.

But why was he such a loner? Axel never went to Higley's, nor hung around the depot. Even with the section gang he hardly ever talked to his crew mates. Just did his job and then went home from the roundhouse at the end of the day. Perhaps it was his deafness? If you can't hear good you don't feel much like talking. But he didn't even go fishing or hunting and you can do those things alone. Why not? Another thing that bothered us that we couldn't understand was that he lived poor. He never had new pair of overalls or a flannel shirt or bandanna handkerchief. Yes, he was ragged both on the job and at home. Maybe he didn't need good clothes for he never went to church or to the school doings, but making the money he did, at least three dollars a day steady and more when he had to work over-time, he could at least have looked half way decent. How come?

It was said that Axel ate poor too, that his dinner bucket rarely had more than a bologna sandwich spread with lard, that and an apple or an onion. How could he do heavy work on such vittles? The clerks at Flinn's store claimed that Axel Erickson never bought meat or eggs or milk or butter or flour or bacon. He did purchase a big hunk of salt pork, some sugar, some lard and a big bag of korpua (a hard Finnish toast) about once a month. No tobacco either nor snuff. How could he live on such stuff? And why? They said the Swede always paid in cash money, usually a lot of small coins, and never asked Mr. Flinn to cash his railroad check. What did he do with that check any-way? His foreman put it in his hand every two weeks, so where did it go?

Perhaps that's why Axel usually took the Saturday afternoon train for Ishpeming every month or so - maybe he had a bank account at the Miner's National there and was saving his money. But for what? Did he have a wife and kids back in Sweden he was supporting and hoped someday to send for them when he had the money? A lot of our people had done that. Yet, if that were true, why didn't he ever get any mail from the old country? Annie Anderson, our postmistress, insisted that he'd never mailed a letter or got one so long as she'd been on the job. Perhaps he had the bank send the money?

And why did Axel seek odd jobs to do even though they paid poor wages? He was our grave digger, the best one our undertaker Ed Stenrud had ever had. "Why," said Ed, "Axel will dig a grave with the corners so true and square, it's a beauty, and he'll do it for a dollar no matter how long it takes him." The Swede was just as good at digging outhouse holes too. No one else would dig an outhouse hole for fifty cents. Why, we asked, would he work so hard for so little? Old man Marchand who hauled the mail sacks from the depot to our post office had a solution. "A fool," he said, "Tout travaillais!" (always working). Few of us were that kind of fool.

Another of the many items that baffled us and kept us speculating was Axel's habit of never taking off his hat, indoors or out, not even on one of our rare hot days when his face ran wet with perspiration. Was it because perhaps he was bald? Or wore a wig? Or had a bad scar on it from that mine accident? A trivial matter, perhaps, but we talked about it.

More important was the fact that Axel kept his doors locked when he was away at work. We didn't like those padlocks. Didn't he trust us? None of us locked our own doors. People just didn't steal in Tioga. Perhaps it was just an old country custom. Perhaps there were more crooks in Sweden. But Axel sometimes kept his doors locked even when he was home as a neighbor found out when she brought him some eggs once when her hens had been laying too many. Insulted, she never did it again. Why would a man lock himself in on purpose? Yes, Axel was a hard man to figure out.

At least Mrs. Johnson had gotten inside Axel's house, and few, if any, of us had ever done so. Alas, she had little to report. "I could tell he didn't want me to come in but I barged right by him and put the bag of eggs on his kitchen table. Axel was polite enough and thanked me but it was clear he wanted me out of there. Only unusual thing was a shoemaker's bench and such stuff in one corner. Pretty bare, that kitchen was, but neat enough. A table, two hard back chairs, a sink, and an awfully old range with kind of rusty pipes going up to the chimney. That's about all. Of course I didn't get to see the other room or the loft."

Early next fall, however, we did get to see more of Axel's place. About nine o'clock one evening, already pitch dark, Charley Olafson, our night watch, saw flames shooting up four feet from Axel's chimney. Fire! Chimney fire! Tioga had heard that cry passed from house to house down the street a lot of times. Men grabbed their sand and salt buckets and an extra pail for well water and ran to the scene. The chemical wagon arrived with four men pulling on the shafts. "Fire! Fire! Up at Axel Erickson's House! Hurry!"

Meanwhile, Charley and Bill Johnson, had banged on Axel's locked door and when nobody answered, they broke it down to enter. Thinking he was sleeping, they ran up the stairs to the loft. No Axel there. Then when they opened the door to the other room off the kitchen, there was the Swede, hunched over a table, playing some kind of a solitaire game next to the one kerosene lamp. He hadn't heard them and they had a hard time getting him to understand that his house was on fire and where the hell was the ladder. Finally Axel understood and said that he didn't have a ladder.

They almost had to pull him out of there too, and he didn't come until he dumped the stuff he was playing with into a pail, covered it with the hat he'd been wearing, and took it outside with him. By that time, other ladders had been brought, men were on the roof, and the bucket brigade was passing along pails of water from the well hand to hand and up the ladders to the men by the flaming chimney. In about fifteen minutes the fire was out. Our people had a lot of practice with chimney fires and this time they'd got it just in time. A little longer and the firey creosote would have cracked holes between the bricks to set the joists or the roof on fire. That would have been it!

Well, as you can imagine, we had plenty to talk about the next day. At least we knew that Axel had hair, blonde hair. But why did he put his hat in the bucket and what did he sweep off the table into it? Some kind of a solitaire game, Charley Olafson had said. When we queried him further on the matter, he just couldn't remember much about it. Axel had a kind of triangle on the table, like those you use to rack up pool balls, and he seemed to be sorting some yellow markers into rows within it. Charley said he didn't pay much attention, being too concerned with trying to tell Axel what was happening and trying to find out where his ladder was. "I saw him this morning too," he said, "and I gave him blue hell for not having a ladder and bucket of sand and salt ready. Told him he ought to know the rule and to go out and buy a ladder right away and to get new stovepipes too. They were cherry red when we got there. I just hope the bugger understood. Those deaf people, they nod even if they don't catch on at all."

Axel must have understood because next morning he went over to Flinn's store to price ladders but didn't buy one, according to Marie who clerked there. He told Flinn thirteen dollars was too much and just walked out. That was a fair price; Axel was just too tight to spend the money. What he did was to go over to Widow Pinault's house where he asked if he could buy the old ladder lying in the grass back of her shed. He'd seen it there when doing some odd jobs for her earlier that summer. Mrs. Pinault said later that she'd told him it was no good for anything but kindling, that her former husband had discarded it because some of the rungs were missing and the others were rotten, Axel could have it free just for carrying it away. "I can fix it," Axel said, and perhaps he tried because that evening Mrs. Johnson saw him put it up against the shed (it was a short ladder), then make his way up the roof to peer down the chimney.

That Saturday was the last time anyone saw Axel alive. We didn't think much about it until Monday when he didn't show up for work at the roundhouse. Probably had the flu or something, though he'd never missed a day's work for years. Perhaps he'd gone on one of his trips to Ishpeming but if so, it was odd no one had seen him walking down the street to the depot. When Tuesday passed and still no sight of the Swede, Mrs. Johnson got up enough nerve to go over. No padlock on the door, so he must be inside. She knocked hard and when no one came, she went inside and searched the house. No Axel, not even in his bed in the loft, so she sent for Charley Olafson.

Charley searched the house too, even went down into the cellar, thinking maybe that perhaps Axel had suffered a stroke or heart attack down there. Then he went out to the barn and shed. The ladder was gone. Finally, he went over to the well and instantly knew what had happened. Peering down into the dark, stone-lined shaft, Charley saw that the bottom rungs of the ladder had broken. Axel must have drowned in the well. Getting the grappling hook from the town hall, the one used to find the body when someone drowned in Lake Tioga, Charley and a couple of other men finally snagged Axel's clothing and pulled him up and out. He'd been dead for several days from the looks of him.

I guess you can imagine how the tongues wagged in Tioga from one end of our village to the other. Why had Axel put that rickety old ladder in the well? Was he cleaning the well? But no, the ladder was too short. It barely reached the water level and when you cleaned a well with a short handled broom and lye water, you first pumped it out and then scrubbed the stones. Besides, we cleaned our wells in the summer when the water level was low, never in late fall when it was high. Charley had said there must have been six feet of water in that well.

Axel must have been after something, though, people said. And the men had found a five foot stick with a hook on one end floating in the water. Yes, he must have been trying to retrieve something, but what? Maybe it was his milk and butter pail. Most of us kept our milk and butter cool by putting them in a pail and lowering it by a rope to the surface of the cold water. Yeah, maybe that was it. There'd been a broken rope hanging from the well frame. Yes, that made sense. Axel had been lowering his milk and butter pail and then when its rope broke, he'd gotten his ladder, nailed it to the well frame, made a stick with a hook on it, and had gone down to fish the pail up. Crazy thing to do but Axel was stingy. He wouldn't want to lose that milk and butter. Sure, he should have boughten a new ladder from Flinn's store, but again he'd been too tight to do so. Doesn't pay to be too stingy. Well, too bad! Axel was a good man. A good worker, he had been.

This explanation for the drowning was about the best we could come up with and most of us felt that it had happened that way. Made pretty good sense. Yet, there were a few pieces of the puzzle that didn't quite fit. For one thing, why would he fish for the milk and butter pail after dark when it would be hard to see; for another, did he really have any milk and butter to lower in that pail? He rarely bought any at the store. Oh well, may he rest in peace.

The talk in Tioga went on to other topics, of shoes and ships and sealing wax and cabbages if not of kings. But it returned to Axel when my father, the village doctor and township supervisor, arranged it with Jim Johnson who took care of the mining properties, to let a very poor family move into Axel's vacant house. The Picottes, who had lived in a tar paper shack down beyond the slaughter house, had sure been unlucky. Henri, the father, had been bedridden for almost two years, first with a bad fracture of the leg, and then by a bad back. My father had done his best and Henri at last was able to cut pulp again. Nevertheless, they were utterly poor, so poor that the township had been providing them monthly with groceries. Moreover, Mrs. Picotee was pregnant again; they needed a break. We helped them move their few pitiful belongings and shared their joy. "Zis house, she is heaven!" exclaimed Henri.

The first thing they had to do, of course, was to clean the well. After all, there'd been a dead body in it for at least three days and nights. Borrowing a good ladder from the Johnson's and some lime and a broom from Mullu's parents, the whole Picotte family went to work with a vengeance. They had to haul up water fast to get ahead of what came in, and they never came to the bottom at that because they found a flour sack tied to a broken rope that contained almost seven thousand dollars in twenty-dollar goldpieces.

And a battered old hat which had seventeen more gold pieces sewn inside its band.

LOST

fellow from Down Below told me the other day that he could always tell when a man was from the U.P. because he always had long, dirty fingernails and no side teeth. I set him straight. I admitted that the lack of side teeth might be correct but how otherwise are you to crack hazelnuts when you're out in the bush? I said that living up here was so unstressful we didn't have to bite our fingernails to the quick. As for the dirt, it was the cleanest dirt in the whole world, all full of minerals, and merely evidence that we weren't afraid to work hard. I told him, too, that I could always tell when a man was from Down Below because he was afraid to leave his car and go ten feet away from the road to take a pee because he was afraid he might get lost. And that he probably would!

Most of us who have loved the forests of the U.P. and wandered them in search of fish or game or just for the hell of it have been lost at one time or another but we do not fear the experience because we know how to cope. Nevertheless, the first time you're really lost is one you'll remember always. I recall mine very vividly. I'd gone up the west branch of the Tioga searching for its origin which turned out to be two little creeks coming out of high swamps and then decided to cut across to the main river which I figured would have been about eight miles away. I'd forgotten to take along my compass (I never forgot again) and it was a dark day, overcast with low clouds, and spitting a drizzling rain. No hint of sun. To hit the main river I knew I had to head southwest and as I left the little source creeks I knew or thought I knew I was hiking in that direction. Three hours later, when I should have been seeing the granite hills along the main river, they weren't there.

Oh there were hills all right, plenty of them, but not the tall ones with rock outcroppings. Perhaps I'd been walking too slowly. Certainly I should be able to find them in another half hour. After walking some more, I climbed to the top of one of the lesser hills and tried to discern the cliffs on the horizon. No! No sign of them.

It was late in the afternoon when I knew I was lost, absolutely, totally lost. Having turned around several times to look over the lay of the land, I didn't even know where I had been or how I'd gotten to where I was. I cursed my negligence in not taking the compass. Any direction could have been north or south or east or west. All I could see looked unfamiliar - and a bit forbidding. I felt the hairs on my neck rising, my heart thumping, and a violent urge to get going, to hurry. But which way should I go? Every direction looked the same. If I picked one by chance, I might end up two days later on the shore of Lake Superior and still be far from civilization. I felt in my pockets. The two pieces of korpua and a sock with coffee grounds in it, were reassuring, but still, there was that panicky urge to get out of there, even to start running. I made myself sit down on a log to smoke a pipe, resolving not to move until it was finished. That should give me time to figure out a sensible solution. The rain rained down on me, and I grinned as I remembered the old English ballad:

> "The wind it bloweth from the north,
> The small rain down doth rain,
> Oh if my love were in my arms,
> And I in my bed again."

That grin helped. I began to think with less emotion. I knew I was south of the divide that separates the watersheds of Lake Superior and Lake Michigan. Any stream I found, no matter how small, would take me south and join the West Branch or the main river. If I had to spend the night in the bush, well that was all right. I'd done it before. Now all I had to do was to find that stream.

It wasn't easy. At first I just wandered around, finding nothing but swamps that seemed to have no outlet. Realizing I might be walking in circles, I decided to make a beeline in one direction only.

Surely it would bring me to flowing water somewhere. But which direction? I picked up a stick, sharpened one end, threw it blindly over my shoulder, then started hiking in the direction it pointed to.

In the U.P. wilderness, it's hard to walk in a straight line because there's always some obstacle to go around. Try as you will, there's a tendency to veer. I knew my own is to veer to the left and I tried to compensate but I never knew how much correction to attempt. So I looked for a large pine or some other landmark in the direction to which my stick had pointed, and for another near where I'd been sitting, then went to the former but always looking back to see where I had been. A sort of leap frog business.

Finally, I found my first flowing stream, a tiny little creek barely a foot wide. But it was flowing up hill! That sounds crazy and it was of course, but that's the way it appeared to me. I had to get down and feel the water to make sure, I was so turned around in my sense of the lay of the land.

Following that little creek was misery, it was so lazy and confused. Sometimes I thought it was as lost as I was but I forced myself to follow it through terrible tangles of alders, through the muck of old beaver dams, through blow-downs of dead tamarack. I was getting very tired and often I fell, once scratching myself on the dead spike of a windfall so badly I had a hard time stopping the bleeding. Keep going! Slug it out! "Even the weariest river winds somewhere safe to sea" I quoted, too pooped to remember its source. Finally I swore that I'd follow that damned creek for only another ten minutes then make camp for the night.

That was enough. Suddenly the little stream led me to a river. What river? It wasn't the Tioga. It was either Wolf Creek or the West Branch. Must be Wolf Creek because it was flowing along the left side of me. But it wasn't because, following it, I saw a pool and a distinctive snag I'd seen going up the West Branch early that morning. Again I sat down on a log to light a pipe. If it were the West Branch, it should be flowing on my right side, not my left. The fact that it was not was almost as hard to accept as seeing that creek flowing uphill. The only explanation that made any sense was that after I had found the sources of the river I'd hiked not southeast toward the main river but had circled west instead. I had followed the little creek to its junction on the west side of the West Branch. If this sounds confusing, it was. Yes, I know how it feels to be lost.

The tendency to circle when walking through the forest is a powerful one. I remember another time in the early spring when I decided to hike to the Huron River which flows out of Lake Tioga to try for walleyes below the dam. Walking along the shoreline, often in snow, when I came to the peninsula that juts out into the lake, I decided to cut across its base, even though it meant crossing a wet swamp full of windfalls to gain some high ground where the walking was easier. Then I came to another swamp almost as bad as the first one and was amazed to find footprints of some other fool who had been doing the same thing. Following them, I finally realized that those footprints were my own. The Finns always made one of their ten foot skis shorter than another to take care of that circling tendency.

I've said that I never went out in the woods again without a compass and that is true. However, in the Iron Range of the Upper Peninsula, there are places where a compass goes nuts. One of them is up by Log Lake and another is in Goochie Swamp west of Tioga. Evidently there are deposits of magnetite in those areas that veer the compass needle away from true north. There's always also a tendency to doubt your compass although I've learned not to do so except in those places. A land looker for Silverthorne and Company always carried two compasses so he would be sure to believe one of them.

I've known a few idiots who say that they don't need a compass, that they can tell by the moss on the trees which way is north. I've never been able to corroborate that. I've seen trees with moss all around them. Where the moss is on one side only it seems to be on the side of the tree opposite the direction of the prevailing wind. Others claim that even on the darkest days you can see a sun shadow if you look hard enough. Perhaps my eyes aren't good enough but certainly you'll see no shadows in the rain. Still others rely on the wind which is usually from the west but there are days when there is no wind and there are days when it comes from other directions.

Besides that essential compass, if you don't want to get lost on a dark or rainy day, the important thing is to know the general lay of the land and the place from which you've started walking. I'm sure the story is apocryphal, and that it has been told elsewhere, but in Tioga the tale runs like this. A landlooker from Silverthorne and Company which owned thousands of acres of forest land in the U.P. once came across Pete Half Shoes snug as a bug in the shell of a large burnt pine, safe from the hordes of mosquitoes that hovered outside a tiny smudge fire. "Are you lost, Pete?" the landlooker asked.

"Naw, Injun no lost. Wigwam lost!" he replied.

Actually, there's a lot of wisdom in that remark. Most people get lost because they don't know where they started from. If you do know, you can always retrace your steps. If you don't you're lost. Following an old logging road or trail, it's easy to lose it. The way to cope with that possibility is to have anchor trees, marked with an axe or knife slash, at the point you can last see the trail clearly. Then you circle around, often stamping the ground, until you find it again. There's a different sound and feel when your feet find the trail even if you can't see it. Off the trail, it's softer and more muffled. I've found my way back to our cabin after dark doing this. Also, at dusk you can often see a faint trail by quickly opening and shutting your eyes. I don't know why this is true but it is. Try it!

Although I loved to roam the forests alone, sometimes only clad in shorts and sneakers, at times sleeping overnight in a lovely spot, I've learned that it isn't really wise to go it alone unless you have to. An experience that brought that home to me most vividly was once when I was looking for gold in the quartz and greenstone studded cliffs between Bushes's Lake and Round Lake. Somehow I fell down one of those cliffs and hit my knee on a sharp rock. Paralyzed, unable to move my leg at all for over an hour, I realized that no one knew where I was or where I had gone. A pretty scary feeling! If I'd had a companion there'd have been no problem. If others had known even approximately where I might have been, they might have found me, but there I was, lost and helpless. Fortunately my leg finally came to life and I was able to limp back to town.

I suppose that one of the best ways of keeping from being lost is to have a guide when you're tackling the wilderness. Once, I had not one guide but two, and we still got lost. Arvo and Arne Mattila had suggested that I go with them to fish a little lake just south of the Huron Mountain Club that was full of big brook trout. They knew where it was because they had trapped the area the fall and spring before. "Full of trout, Cully," they said. "Jumping like crazy every night." So of course I went with them.

We started at the Haysheds on the Tioga and walked northeast all afternoon through rough country. When I suggested we stop to boil a pot of coffee and eat, they said no, that we'd wait till we came to the lake. Just before dusk, Arvo said, "Arne, you're lost. That lake ain't the way you're going. We gotta go this way."

Arne argued and Arvo argued, and they disagreed. Finally Arvo got mad. "I know!" he yelled. "Cully, you come with me. I show you lake."

"No!" said Arne. "Arvo, you crazy. Cully, you come with me."

Arvo headed west and Arne headed east. With the wisdom of Solomon within me for once, I followed Arne. He had the packsack containing the grub.

And finally he did find the lake with Arvo on its shoreline.

ARMINDA

Arminda adopted us when she was only six weeks old. Dad brought her to our kitchen in a little wooden box inside a burlap sack and told my mother, grinningly, that he had a present for her. Pulling off the bag and opening the box, he pointed to the little pink piglet that lay quietly therein. But not for long! Opening first one little slanted eye and then the other, suddenly the baby pig tore out of its box and raced all around the kitchen floor squealing at the top of its little lungs.

For a moment Mother stood there transfixed and then she climbed on a chair. "No! No, John. Get that creature out of here! I'll not have a pig in my house. Do you think I'm Bridget Murphy? Take it out this very minute!" She was weeping with fury.

Dad saw she was beyond reasoning with so he and I finally corralled the piglet, put it back in its box and bag and took it out to the horses' box stall in the barn. When he returned, Dad explained.

"It's payment on a bill, Edyth," he said. "I delivered Pete Fontaine's wife last February and he couldn't pay me then. Out of work ever since, being in debt has been bothering him. He's a proud man, so today he brought me the little shoat. It's just been weaned from the sow, he said, and may need a little extra care for a time. I just couldn't refuse Pete. Can't you understand?"

Mother had calmed down. "Yes, I understand," she said. "And I also know you've alway had a mind to raise a pig, though goodness knows we've enough animals to take care of - two horses, one cow, one dog, and all those chickens. I feel sorry for Cully knowing he'll have to take care of them."

"Oh that's all right," I said. "That pig's fun." She sure was, too. I played with her most of the afternoon after laying down a big carpet of fresh straw in the box stall. She'd even play hide and seek with me, burrowing herself in a pile of straw with only her pink nose sticking out, then come out squealing when I tickled her hind end.

But she wouldn't eat. I put out saucers of warm milk and even made her some Cream of Wheat and toast but the little pig wouldn't touch them. Nor did she drink any water. Finally I brought her into the kitchen again and asked mother for help. After giving me a piece of her mind but feeling sorry for the little thing, she found a baby bottle with a nipple and filled it with warm milk laced with a bit of molasses. Then, when she saw how awkward I was, she picked up the piglet in her arms, put the nipple in its mouth, and crooned to it as though it were a baby. Well, the little pig immediately began sucking and making little gurgling noises of contentment until it finally fell asleep. Mother was hooked. "Go get its box, Cully and put it behind the kitchen range. But just for tonight, mind you! It's going to be a cold night and if the horses come in from the barnyard, they might step on her."

That's the way it went for over two weeks until the weather warmed up and my father built the pigpen and pig house beside our chicken yard. Before then during the day, the pig lived in the barn or played with me in the grass by our back steps while at night it slept in its box behind the stove. I've never had so much fun with any pet. It loved attention and would yelp a chorus of delighted oinks every time I took it out of the barn to chase me or to be chased on the back lawn. Sometimes I'd lie down in the grass and the pig would climb over me or nuzzle my bare arms or neck. Never tried to bite me; just wanted to play. And how she loved to eat. By first putting the baby nipple smeared with mush in a dish of the cereal, the piglet was soon eating out of a pan, and finally drinking out of another one. Sometimes, after having had her fill, she'd dump over the pan of water and roll in it yelping to high heaven.

Now my father was a fine physician but a lousy carpenter. Never could he saw a board straight across or hit a nail without bending it, so both the V-shaped pig house he built and the fence he erected next to the chicken yard were hardly works of art. Nor were they very functional. I'd bet we repaired that fence thirty times while Arminda was with us.

But I should tell you how she happened to get her name. My father had a patient named Arminda Latour whom he thoroughly detested. Neurotic and hypochondriac and demanding, she was always inventing a new set of symptoms. Moreover, she kept a filthy house - not fit for any decent pig, Dad said, let alone a human. Well, one day shortly after our piglet had joined our family, Dad had been out all night on a tough baby case, had made house calls all morning, and had treated many patients in his office that afternoon. Just as he had gotten to sleep on the couch word was sent up that Arminda Latour was dying and to come right away. Of course he went right down to see her.

As he told the story to us later, he found the woman lying in bed, clutching her fat belly, moaning and screaming. Dad examined her heart and pulse. Completely normal. He felt around for signs of appendicitis. None. Gall bladder? No! What had she eaten for dinner? Only three pasties, she said. It was just a big, well deserved bellyache. Dad gave her a big slug of castor oil and some calomel and came wearily home. So that was why he named our pig Arminda. "When that pig grows up and becomes a hog and we butcher it I'll eat every damned morsel of Arminda with relish," he said.

The name Arminda was too hard to use so first we called her Minda and finally "Minnie." Minnie Gage.

We transferred Minnie to her new quarters after dark, carrying her in her bedbox and putting it inside the V-shaped pig house within the pen. Whether Lord Fauntleroy, our Rhode Island Red rooster, awoke Minnie I don't know but shortly after dawn I heard the damndest squealing below my window. Arminda had climbed the steps of the back shed and was sitting there yelling for breakfast. Well, I fixed her a panful and, oinking all the way, she followed me to the pen to eat lustily while I staked down Dad's wire fence where she'd lifted it to get out. I think I had to fix that fence every day for a month until I buried the bottom ends of some boards all around its circumference.

Don't tell me pigs aren't smart. Pigs are a lot smarter than dogs, yes, and horses too. Once, when I was staking down the fence again and wasn't looking, Minnie hid two of the stakes under the straw of her house, and she soon learned how to lift off the loop of wire that shut her gate.

Another time, after I'd gotten some more heavy fencing and made her pen hog-tight, I just couldn't figure out how Minnie was escaping.

The fence was all right, the gate was securely locked, but again and again Minnie was at our back door or rooting in Mother's vegetable garden. Indeed one morning the pig plowed up a whole row of beets that were just ready for canning. Dad checked everything and couldn't see how Minnie had managed it. "Wait a minute!" he said. Maybe the bugger..." and then he led me to the place outside the corner of the fence, the corner where Minnie's V-shaped house sat. There in the earth were the deep prints of her hooves. Minnie had run up the side of her house to leap over the fence. Of course, we moved the pig house to the middle of her yard and then had some morning peace for a while.

By summer's end, however, Minnie had developed a new strategy for seeing the wide, wide world outside her pen. She'd wait there just inside the gate looking innocent as hell as I unlocked it to bring her the pails of food and water. Then just as I edged my way in, Minnie would charge out, often knocking over the pails or me as she did so. Usually she high-tailed it over to our house or barn or garden and played around there until hungry enough to follow a new slop pail of stuff back to the pen if I coaxed her enough. That damned pig played games with me day after day.

I said that Minnie usually stayed fairly near our place after getting out but there were some instances when she roamed afar. Once she broke down the Salo's pig fence and cavorted around with their full grown hogs for an entire afternoon before deciding that she preferred people to pigs. Another time, early in the fall, she followed the kids to school and hung out in the schoolyard until she could follow them home. Minnie loved kids, and when she heard them going down the street she'd start squealing so loud they'd often come to her yard and scratch her with a stick to hear Minnie grunt her thanks. What she preferred, however, for the scratching was a sharp edged board. It almost made her purr.

Because it was one of my chores to feed and take care of Minnie my father was frequently mad at me when she won at the gate game and escaped. I don't think he understood how clever she was until he had to take the slop pail over to her once when I was sick. Minnie made a monkey of him, feinting one way, then bolting through his legs. She was gone two days that time, and I began to fear (or hope) that the bears had gotten her when old man Marchand came to Dad's office and said, "Doctaire, your couchon blanche, ze peeg, she is in my cellaire." How she got down in that root cellar, we never could figure out, and by the time Dad finally got her home he was mad as a hatter. "She won't lead and she won't drive. Sure gave me a bad time," he said. I couldn't help grinning.

Speaking of bears, one of them almost got Minnie one night. Next morning we saw bear tracks all around her pen and the bear had torn down the fence on one side almost completely. Perhaps it was Minnie's long practice in zigzagging that saved her soul or hide but

44

somehow she managed to flee to our back steps where she started squealing so loudly, Dad came out and scared the bear away with a shotgun blast. Then he couldn't get the terrified Minnie even to enter our barn. Minnie wanted the safety of our kitchen and finally Dad in desperation let her in. Minnie was a big pig by then too. No, she was already a hog. Anyway, Mother sure had a fit next morning when she came down to make the breakfast coffee.

There was good reason for Minnie's getting so big. Never did a pig enjoy eating as much as Minnie did. It was really fun to watch her at the trough, grunting and chewing her way from one end of it to the other, sometimes letting out a huge squeal of sheer pleasure. Two or three times a day she ate everything we brought. Minnie's slop pail was always in our kitchen corner and nothing went to the garbage pile except tin cans or bottles. She had everything else. Dad had corn shipped up from Ishpeming but her main course was always milk and middlings (bran). Minnie ate the suckers I caught in the creek, the potatoes whose sprouts were too long to plant, the rotting eggs of a hen that had hidden its nest. Once she broke into the chicken yard and terrified the squawking hens but only ate their chicken feed, not the fowls themselves. In the Mad Moon of October when partridge go crazy, one of them killed itself in the chicken wire and Minnie ate it, feathers and all. She loved bones of any kind, the bigger the better. Hearing Minnie crunch those bones gave me the shudders. What if they had been my leg!

Throughout all the months that Minnie had been with us Dad had been remembering the pork of his youth on the farm. Store bought bacon, he said, never really had the savor of the bacon his father had hanging in his smokehouse. Now, in November, whenever he saw Arminda my father eyed her with anticipation. "There are four good slabs of bacon there," he'd say. "And two fine hams, and porkchops, and scrapple, and headcheese, and, if I can find someone who knows how to cure 'em some pickled pigs feet. Ah, we'll have some good eating."

Such talk sure didn't appeal to me, nor to my mother, nor to my little brother and sister. We all swore we couldn't and wouldn't eat a bite of Minnie. Why it was cannibalism. She was a member of the family. Even when Mother said she wouldn't use Minnie's lard and so he wouldn't be getting any pie, my father brushed it off. "No point getting sentimental about a critter. Pork's pork. You'll eat it when it's on the table." Then Dad found a man who would butcher Minnie and smoke the meat when the weather got cold enough. We kids sure watched the thermometer, hoping that Indian Summer would last forever.

It didn't. When the first snow arrived, Dad told us that the next day would be Minnie's last. We cried and implored him but to no avail. Like all the other kids in Tioga I'd seen a lot of butchering done.

I knew how the man would hit Minnie between the eyes with a sledge and cut her throat and all the rest of the gory details. I didn't sleep much that night.

The next morning when the man appeared with his sledge and other stuff Dad asked me to show him where Minnie was. I could hardly bring myself to obey and as soon as I did I fled back to the house preparing myself for her death squeals.

But in a few moments, the man came to the door again. "Doctor," he said. "I can't butcher that hog. She's pregnant and I guess she'll be having her pigs in a week or two. The meat's not fit to eat now and it would be a shame not to let you keep those baby pigs. Call me again about two months after they've been weaned."

Dad never did. He gave Minnie to a poor family in town. "I guess one pig in a lifetime is enough for us." It was!

A BIT OF HARMONY

I t all started when Bill and Jim Trevarrow were cutting swamp hay down by the Beaver Dam and found that they could harmonize. One of those perfect U.P. mornings in late June with fat white clouds swimming lazily across a very blue sky. It was very good to be alive! The scythes were sharp and suddenly in time with their swish Bill couldn't help breaking into song. "Wait till the sun shines, Nellie," he sang. His brother joined him: "When the clouds go drifting by..." but in two part harmony. Jim hadn't planned to do it. Just happened. They looked at each other in amazement. "Hey, that's pretty good! Let's try'er again."

Both young men had fine voices that blended smoothly, Bill's was a strong baritone and Jim's a high clear tenor. They gave poor Nellie quite a beating as they took turns singing the melody or the harmony and often they had to stop to search for the note they wanted before they got it right. They monkeyed around with the notes of the scale: *Doh* and *me* and *sol* jibed good, but *me* and *fah* sure didn't. "Look, Jim," said the older brother. "I'll sing *doh, me, sol, doh* going up and you sing *doh, sol, me, doh* coming down. Yep, that works. How about *doh, fah, lah?*" Before the morning was over, they had explored many chords - and cut a lot of hay.

At noon Bill and Jim almost hated to go back to the log cabin at their homestead for dinner. It had been a glorious morning and they dreaded their father's depressing sourness. Hell to live with, he was, even before their mother died and worse afterwards. The brothers would have been long gone to other parts but they had promised to take care of the old man. Al Trevarrow had reason for his bitterness, I guess, because his right arm was completely paralyzed and he had a gimpy leg, both resulting from an accident in the mine. Some timber lagging had given way resulting in a minor avalanche of rock that had almost buried him. Every painful step Al took as he did the cooking and minor chores around the house was accompanied by his cursing the Oliver Mining Company or his boys, or the beans in the pot. Old Al Trevarrow nursed his bitterness to keep it hot.

The Trevarrow boys had once discussed getting the hell out and letting the county put their father in the poorhouse but somehow they just couldn't. The forty acres they had cleared and destumped provided enough potatoes, rutabagas, and beans to last them through the winter and these with fish and game made up most of their sustenance. The Trevarrows also had a cow, chickens, occasionally a pig, and Maude, an ancient horse whose ribs slatted its hide. Al Trevarrow never fed Maude enough. There was a saying in Tioga that every Fourth of July the old man would give Maude a handful of oats and say, "Here, eat till ye bust!"

For their necessaries, sugar, flour, salt, coffee and tobacco, the Trevarrows relied on Al's mining pension of ten dolars a month and on the money that Bill and Jim earned cutting pulpwood during the winters. It was understood that they always gave half of their earnings to the old man who stashed the money away in empty Peerless tobacco pails which he kept under his bed. It was bad for the boys when their winter money ran out and they had to ask him for some to buy their evening bottles of beer at Higley's saloon.

At noon when the boys got back to the cabin they were sweaty so they washed up, using the white cracked enamel wash basin on the bench outside the cabin door to hold the water they dipped from the rain barrel under the eaves. Only a sliver of yellow Fels Naptha laundry soap was left but they shared it, and after the spluttering was over, they dried their faces, arms, and shoulders on the flour sack hanging from its nail. Still full of the morning's joy, their faces fell when they entered the dark hot cabin. Beans, salt pork, and smashed rutabagas again! Their father noticed. "Well, why don't you get some work and bring us something better. Eat it now or have it for supper! How much hay you cut?"

"Oh, maybe half an acre," said Jim.

"Hell, when I was a lad your age I could cut an acre a morning and never know I had a back." Al went to cursing the Oliver Iron Mining Company again. The brothers ate swiftly and then got the hayrakes and pitchforks from the barn. It was good to be back in the sunshine again.

On their way to the Beaver Dam meadow, they stopped to cut a basswood limb from which they whittled pegs to replace the missing tines of their home-made hay rakes. Then, putting the rakes in water so the pegs would swell tightly, the boys toppled over a slim dead tamarack sapling and set it up in the meadow to hold the haystack. Swamp hay is very nutritious but only if it is properly cured. Horses prefer timothy, and cows clover, but both can do well enough on swamp hay alone.

As they began raking the previous day's cutting and carrying it to the stack pole, Bill Trevarrow suddenly sang the Nellie song again:

> "Wait till the sun shines, Nellie,
> While the clouds go drifting by,
> We will be happy, Nellie,
> Don't you cry.
> Down Lover's Lane we'll wander,
> Sweetheart, you and ..."

"Dammit, Jim," he said. "When you harmonize on 'I' you sing 'sol' and it isn't right. It should be 'tee'. Let's try it, sweetheart, you and I.' Yeah, yeah, yeah. That's it; that's lots better!" He slapped his brother on the back in congratulation. "But to hell with Nellie. How about "Down By the Old Mill Stream?"

There was a lot of hay to stack around the pole and it had to be done carefully. You don't just heap it up; you flip your pitchfork so the stems slant downward, layer upon layer. That way, if it rains, and in the U.P. it can rain suddenly at any time, the water will run off. You can leave a stack around a pole all winter and have good hay in the spring if you built it right.

By the end of haying week the boys had cocked five stacks and had mastered three more songs: "In the Shade of the Old Apple Tree," "Every Little Movement Has a Meaning of Its Own," and "Daisy, Daisy, Give Me Your Answer True." To celebrate, they took some of their beer money and went down Tioga's long hill street to Higley's saloon. They sure were feeling good and soon felt even better.

I should tell you about Higley's saloon because it, with the school, churches, and railroad station, were about the only places where our men could socialize a bit. A false-front frame structure by the railroad tracks, it had been built during the 1880's to serve and fleece the iron miners and lumberjacks. At one time our village of Tioga had five other saloons plus a red whorehouse but after all the white pine forest had been cut and the mines closed down all of them folded. Not Higley's. Even when a fire consumed most of it, rebuilding occurred immediately. Most of us were relieved. Without a good saloon a town died.

Higley's was a good saloon. Almost as old as the Douglass House (Dog House) in Houghton or the Antlers at the Soo, its long bar had been polished by the elbows of many nationalities. Behind the bar was a long beveled mirror that distortedly reflected the faces of the drinkers as well as the large variety of whiskey bottles stacked before it. These were strictly ornamental as a traveler from Down Below discovered when he told Higley, the proprietor, that he'd have a slug of that Old McNeish over there. Higley slid the bottle over to him with a shot glass and said, "Help yourself!" A great burst of laughter from the men in the saloon greeted the traveler's discovery that the bottle like all the others was empty.

"You want whiskey, I give you whiskey," said Higley. "Them fancy bottles been empty for fifty years."

Along the wall opposite the bar were five booths, each of which could hold four or five drinkers and there were also four tables with wire soda fountain chairs where men could play cards if their money held out. House rule number one was that you had to buy a drink every hour or get out. If you bought more than one in the first hour you could sit longer as you nursed the last one. Higley ran a tight ship. He wouldn't serve boys or women or anyone so polluted he couldn't stand on one leg for thirty seconds. No fighting inside the saloon but it was OK outside. A big man, Higley could handle anything. Above his dirty apron he had muscles on the muscles of his bare arms. When Higley tended bar, wearing his brown derby that otherwise hung on a huge set of antlers next to Slimber Jim's great stuffed trout, he was all business. At the first sign of trouble Higley's fierce blue-black mustache would begin to quiver then Pow! He could jump over the bar, slug the bugger and heave him out the front door faster than you could say spit.

Before Bill and Jim Trevarrow went to the saloon, according to their custom, they "pushed out the St. Paul train." A lot of our towns-people did that. It wasn't just something to do; it was a chance to get a glimpse of another world. The brightly lit dining car with its linen and red rose on each table, the black sleeping car porters greeting new passengers that had come up from Marquette or Ishpeming to take the train to Chicago, the baggage and freight being loaded up front, the railway mail clerks deftly slinging letters into various boxes in the mail car, all these sights fascinated all of us. They meant that there truly were horizons beyond the confines of our tight little isolated village of Tioga.

When the last "All aboard" had been shouted and with a great burst of white steam and whistle blowing, the train pulled out, Jim and Bill walked over to the saloon to spend the last of their beer money. All the regulars were there when they went through the slotted swinging doors. Slimber Jim Vester, our town liar, was telling a stranger his bear story. Pete Half-Shoes, our resident Indian, was slumped in his corner of the last booth, smelling slightly of Mabel, his pet skunk and bed partner. Sven Anderson at the bar was spitting at the brass spittoon between beer gulps and hitting it every time. Eino Tuomi and his friend Emil Olson were arguing about the palatability of deer nuts. Billy Bones was sitting on a stool mumbling his temperance lecture to himself. Laf Bodine, our King of the Poachers, was telling Old Man McGree how his Uncle Joe had fooled the game warden. Yes, most of the regulars were there along with six or seven other men.

Bill and Jim went up to the bar and plunked down their money but Higley said, "Wait a minute, boys. I gotta light the lamps. It's getting dark." He got a tall stool and went over to the old wagon wheel chandelier that hung from the ceiling near the pot-bellied stove. The word "Wait" hit the boys at the same time and to the amazement of all, they began to sing. "Wait Till the Sun Shines, Nellie," they harmonized. Higley stopped dead in his tracks with the lighted match in his hand. "Hey," he said. "That's damned good! Sing it again!" They did and most of the men clapped or stamped their feet. As Higley put out the beer for them, he was thinking hard.

"You boys able to sing some other tunes like that?" he asked "Had a fiddler come in here once and business sure picked up. Trouble was, we all got damned sick of Turkey in the Straw." The Trevarrows obliged with "Down at the Old Mill Stream" and then "It's a Hot Time in the Old Town Tonight," all in close harmony. Higley and the other men in the saloon were entranced, and they showed it. "More! More!" they yelled. "No, that's enough," said Jim. "We've got to drink our beer and get home." Before they left, Higley told them that if they'd come back next night and sing some more he'd set them up with free beer. Walking up our hill street that night with the applause still ringing in their ears, Bill and Jim sure felt good. Free beer too! They sang all the way back home.

You must remember that this took place at the turn of the century, long before phonographs or TV or radio had come to Tioga. About the only singing heard in our village was in church or when children obediently tackled "Row, Row, Row Your Boat Gently Down the Stream" in school, or when some mother comforted her baby with a lullaby. There was a lot of talking done in Tioga but very little singing.

The Trevarrow boys made a real change. Night after night as they harmonized up and down our street our people enjoyed their concerts. We'd sit on our porches or steps at dusk listening to the harmony coming down the board sidewalks then fading out as the boys passed. At times, especially on their way back from Higley's they'd stop at one place or another to sing several songs, usually opposite the Catholic Church or in front of Mr. Donegal's (Old Blue Balls) house or my father's hospital or the Town Hall.

Gradually Jim and Bill Trevarrow increased their repertoire, remembering the old songs their mother had sung so often. Mrs. Trevarrow was a singing woman. Welsh by descent, she had made her days down there on the homestead bearable by song. The Welsh are a singing race by nature so perhaps that is where the boys got their talent. Anyway, they'd sure heard from her a lot of songs that now they tried to recall: Annie Laurie, In the Shade of the Old Apple Tree, Down in the Valley, the Valley so Low, I Want a Girl Just Like the Girl that Married Dear Old Dad, Old Dog Tray Ever Faithful, Old Black Joe, My Old Kentucky Home, In the Gloaming - oh, there were a lot more. Often the boys would have trouble remembering some of the words but never the melodies and once they'd sing them several times the words came back.

By the end of July month, the whole town of Tioga was singing as it had never sung before. High School couples were doing it too as they walked at twilight under the big maples hand in hand. Mothers sang more to their babies. Why I even heard Mr. Salo singing the old Finnish folk song Kuopia as he ground down an old file to make a puukka (knife). The melody was in a minor key and the words he sung sounded like this: "Mikksi tau tu sineh O Lempia, Mikksi tau tu Raukusta." I didn't know what they meant but they sounded good and the old Finn sure looked happy.

Then something occurred that opened new vistas to Bill and Jim. The train from the Copper Country was late one evening and they were sitting far down the station platform on a baggage truck rehearsing some new songs they planned to sing at Higley's later. "Down in the valley/the valley so low/Hang your head over/Hear the wind blow/ Roses love sunshine/Violets love dew/Angels in heaven/know I love you" It was getting dark and they were sure surprised when a passenger came up behind them and joined in. "The name's Flanagan," he said. "Hope you boys don't mind my woodshedding." They were delighted. His was a rich bass voice with a remarkable range and the new addition to the harmonizing made the old song sound thrice as good.

"You boys have fine voices," Flanagan said. "Haven't heard any better for a long time and I've been singing in barbershop quartets down in Green Bay for years. Why don't you get yourselves a second tenor and a bass and have a quartet of your own? I come through here about every two weeks on my rounds selling hardware for Keene and Williams wholesale house and the U.P. is now my territory. But to hell with talking, let's try "Cuddle Up a Little Closer, Lovey Mine." Its got a silly lyric but it's catchy and easy to harmonize on."

"Cuddle up a little closer, Lovey mine,
How'd you like to be my little clinging vine,
Like to see your cheeks so rosy,
Like to hold you comfy-cosy,
Cause I love from head to toe-sy,
Lovey Mine."

Before his train came in and he left for Green Bay, Flanagan had given the boys so many suggestions and pointers their heads were reeling. He taught them to hang onto that final note of a phrase shifting from one chord to another until hitting it. He opened their ears to chords they had never thought of. Altogether it was an experience that shook them up so much they didn't even sing at Higley's that night.

Nor the next night either. Somehow, a lot of the joy seemed to have gone out of their duets. Remembering the rich harmony when Flanagan had sung bass with them, the harmony in the duet seemed thin and incomplete. The whole town missed the evening music at dusk, wondering what had happened. Higley sent word to tell them he'd give them not only free beer but fifty cents each night if they'd come back but they tried it once and could hardly bear the sound of their voices. The salesman was right. They had to form a quartet.

Finding a second tenor wasn't too difficult. They remembered that Raoul Deroche had once sung along with them in the saloon when he really got liquored up and that he had a clear true voice. A shy man, it took some liquid persuading to get him to form a trio. He couldn't harmonize worth a damn though. Had no knack for it at all, but Raoul could sing the melody true. That was good enough because Jim and Bill were thereby freed to sing different notes in the harmonizing. After practicing a few times at Raoul's house, the three of them felt brave enough to try the saloon again. They sure got a good reception. Why Higley was so entranced he gave them each a dollar.

But it wasn't enough. They needed a bass, a good deep in the belly bass voice. Flanagan, on another of his trips, told them so, and demonstrated how much it would mean by singing with their trio down at the station. Lord Almighty, down there by the railroad tracks the four blended voices sounded as though they came from heaven when Flanagan added his boom-boom harmony to the others singing My Wild Irish Rose.

But how do you find someone who can sing bass in a little forest town like Tioga where you rarely if ever hear a man sing? Jim and Bill kept listening everywhere for a deep speaking voice, hoping that its owner might also be able to carry a tune. Joe Beaudreau seemed to be a possibility at first. His voice was low enough all right and he liked his beer but he was sure a slow learner. In fact he never could remember any of the words of the songs they tried to teach him so they had Joe just act like a bass drum and sing "Pom, Pom, Pompom, Pom" sounding out the rhythm in his deep voice. But even then he forgot his lines and began singing "Chuga Lug, Bug, Bug" so they had to drop him.

Recalling that old Billy Simonds, a retired Cornish miner, used to belt out the hymns when the boys still went to Sunday School, they called at his house one Saturday afternoon. Knowing that

Billy was a Godfearing churchman and perhaps a teetotaler, they said nothing about Higley's beer but asked him to help them remember the words of some of the old hymns like "When the Roll is Called Up Yonder" and "Let the Lower Lights be Burning."

"Ah, me boys. Come in, Come in and I'll sing 'em for ye." He led them into the parlor and picked out the tunes on a wheezy old organ with one finger. Old Billy had a fine bass voice and they had a fine old time but when the boys proposed that he join them to form the quartet and sing down at Higley's he was outraged and showed them the door.

Thus thwarted, the trio decided to make the best of it by having Bill do all his harmonizing at the lowest part of his baritone range hoping thereby to approximate the effect of a bass voice. That required a lot of practice which at first they did at Raoul's house. But it didn't work out for a lot of reasons including the fact that Raoul had three kids under five plus a hound that kept howling off key whenever they sang.

After considerable discussion and with some misgivings they told their father all about their singing down at Higley's and asked him if he'd mind if they brought Raoul down to the homestead to work up some new songs. "You mean that Higley gives you free beer just for singing?" The old man was incredulous. "Why, he never gave out a free beer in his life. What kind of songs you singing down there? Dirty ones, I bet." No, they said. Just the old sweet songs their mother used to sing. They demonstrated:

> "Just a song at twilight, when the lights are low,
> And the flickering shadows softly come and go;
> Though the heart be weary, sad the day and long,
> Still to us at midnight..."

The father stopped them. "No," he growled. "Not 'midnight.' It's 'twilight' and then in a deep bass voice the boys had never heard before he sang: "Still to us at *twilight* comes love's old sweet song. Comes love's old sweet song." "Yeah, boys. That was your mother's favorite. We used to sing it together when we was a-courting." There was a hint of tears in his eyes.

The boys had found the fourth member of their barbershop quartet but they didn't bring it up to their father until after several sessions of practice and only when they found that he not only was enjoying their harmonizing but occasionally could not help joining them. They told him how much Flanagan's bass voice had improved the sound and how hard they'd been hunting for someone who had one. It took a lot of persuading but in the end, and only after they took him down to Higley's to see for himself that indeed there was free beer, did their father say he would give it a trial.

The weeks thereafter were a delight. The whole atmosphere down at the homestead changed. Why, there were entire days that Al Trevarrow even forgot to cuss the Oliver Iron Mining Company. There's something about close harmony that is contagious, I guess. It spreads from the singing to all the rest of your living.

Anyway, after several weeks of daily practice at the homestead, the four men felt confident enough about their singing together to give Higley's a try. They also had a lot of new songs because Al Trevarrow had remembered them, songs like Old Black Joe, I Want A Girl Just Like the Girl That Married Dear Old Dad, Swing Lo, Sweet Chariot, The Last Rose of Summer, Alouette, (Raoul sure liked that last one) After the Ball Was Over and Casey Would Waltz With the Strawberry Blonde as the Band Played On. Oh, they had a lot of songs now and when the quartet stood there together at the bar and belted them out in full voice, the saloon almost went crazy with delight. "Yeah, Yeah!" the drinkers shouted. "Wahoo!" When Higley who was Irish from the Ould Sod, heard them sing "I'll Take You Home Again, Kathleen" it hit him so hard he yelled "Drinks on the House!" Never, in the long history of the saloon, had those words ever been uttered there before.

About ten o'clock Al Trevarrow muttered to his sons that it was time to quit and go home. He'd had three beers, three free beers, and was getting tired. Never had he known such a fine evening, he said but enough was enough. They'd come back another night. Higley offered them each a silver dollar if they'd sing another hour and when they refused, he gave it to them anyway.

I'd bet though that Higley must have been a bit upset when about half of his customers followed the quartet up our hill street begging for another song. Resting for a moment against the iron fence in front of old Blue Ball's house, the four of them surrendered with Joshua Fought the Battle of Jericho. Great applause and yells of approval! When other people joined the procession, in front of my Dad's hospital, the quartette gave them "Auld Lang Syne" thinking it would end their entreaties for just one more. But it didn't and by the time they got to our Town Hall half of Tioga was following them.

"Three more and that's it, dammit!" shouted Bill. The first song was "Harvest Moon," a fine one for harmonizing, then "I've Got a Gal Just Like the Gal Who Married Dear Old Dad." By this time the whole crowd was singing with them - even Aunt Lizzie who flatted a high note so badly someone put a fat hand over her mouth.

Bill raised his hands above his head until the crowd grew still. "OK," he said. "We'll sing you one last song: 'Good Night Ladies' and all of you join in as I wave the beat."

> "Good night, ladies,
> Good night, ladies,
> Good night, ladies,

We're off to leave you now.
Merrily we roll along
To the deep blue sea."

Dropping off Raoul at his house, the three Trevarrow men walked down the old logging road to their homestead closely side by side.

THE GREEN RIBBON

I was a senior in high school when Mullu asked me if I'd like to go with him to old lady Pukkinen's barn dance. "She holds it every Saturday night," he said, "and you've never seen anything like it. Real backwoods U.P. stuff with a fiddler, drummer, and an accordian player, most of them half drunk. Always a good fight or two but they're outside. Olga Pukkinen and her son pitch them out of the loft as soon as they start something. Lots of Finn girls to dance with."

It was Maytime after a hard winter and because my glands were beginning to work I foolishly said yes. However, as Mullu and I walked the five miles to the barn I began to doubt my judgment. I wasn't much of a dancer. I could waltz without tripping and could do a two-step if I had to but that was about it. Mullu grinned in the twilight. "All they do mainly is the polka," he said, "but they sure kick up their heels. The girls will teach you fast. Most of the men there can't dance either. Just hold the girl and stamp your feet in time with the accordian. Nothing to it!"

As we approached the big barn and its two outbuildings, Mullu filled me in a bit further. "That first shed there is the booze shed. That's where old lady Pukkinen's son hands out his moonshine for fifty cents a snort. I don't recommend it, Cully. Even diluted with the old gal's red soda pop it's awful. He makes it out of potatoes, they say, but it sure has a wallop. Also, Cully, if a girl asks you to dance, and they will, don't say no or she'll slap your face good and hard. And if some big Finn cuts in while you're dancing, let him or you'll be in big trouble. Most of the fights start that way. Just walk off and sit down." I wished I were home in bed.

We climbed some rickety stairs to the loft where the music had already begun although no dancers were yet on the floor. At one corner of the big room about twelve or thirteen girls and women sat on hay bales and in the other corner stood about the same number of young men. The three musicians were on a little platform between the two groups.

I'd hardly taken in the sight when Mullu pushed me forward to where old lady Pukkinen herself sat in a chair behind a table. A big woman, a powerful woman, she looked me over carefully. "You want dance? Fifty cents. You want green ribbon, two dollars?" she roared in a surprisingly strong voice. Mullu hadn't said anything about a green ribbon so I answered that I wanted to dance. When I put down the money the woman grabbed my arm, slid up my sleeve and pounded a rubber stamp on the back of my wrist. While Mullu was also getting stamped I tried to read it. A circular stamp mark, on its periphery it bore the words "City of Chicago" and in the center were the letters O.K. When Mullu and I joined the group of men he explained. "If you have to go out to pee or want a shot of moonshine, that stamp means you can come in again without paying twice. Don't know where she got that second hand stamp."

As the trio began their second number, another rousing polka, Madam Pukkinen cupped her hands and yelled, "OK, you sunsbitses, dance! You no come here for look or hear moosik. You come for dance, so dance!"

Three or four of the young men went over to the hay bales, got their partners and started stomping and kicking as the couples whirled around the floor. Mullu was one of them and his partner was a cute little blonde. He winked at me as he went past, seeing that I had edged my way toward the rear of the group of men. I sure felt helpless and alone. One of the men told me that his feet hurt. "I been wearing clompers all winter," he said. "Feet spread; shoes too tight now."

Mullu returned at the end of the number. "See, Cully," he grinned. "Nothing to it! Wait till things start jumping." I asked him who the three girls were who sat by themselves and had green ribbons in their hair.

"Oh, those are the Pukkinen girls, sisters. The old gal's their mother and she calls them her bread and butter. Maybe you'll find out why. Anyway, watch what happens next."

The drummer had returned from somewhere down below and

as the band started playing again, the three Pukkinen sisters marched across to where we stood, picked out their victims, and danced off. Then some of the other girls came up to us. "You want dance?" Most of the men they asked said sure but one said no. Mullu had briefed me correctly. The rejected girl swung a haymaker and caught him right smack in the face. He just grinned.

When the rejected girl went back to her group on the hay bales another took her place, got rejected and slapped the fellow hard. Then another and another girl did same thing to the same man until finally he gave in and said yes. Mullu was enjoying the sight. "Okkari does that every night," he said. "I think he likes having the girls hit and it gives him a chance to get the one he wants." I resolved, however, after seeing some of the wallops Okkari got that I for one would not say no.

I didn't have to wait long. Over walked the cute little blonde Mullu had danced with. Brushing past the other men behind whom I was hiding, she made directly for me. "You want to dance with me, Cully?" she asked smilingly and before I knew it I was on the floor cavorting around. "Mullu told me your name," she laughed, "and he said you were shy. I like shy ones." I apologized for my awkwardness, saying that I'd never done the polka before. "That's OK," she replied. "Lempi will teach you. I'm Lempi." She did too and by the time Mullu claimed her again after two numbers I was really enjoying myself. There's something about doing the polka that gets rid of all inhibitions. You whirl the girl around and kick up your outside foot, and you stomp and jump, and just let 'er go Gallegher. Wahoo! I didn't yell wahoo like the others did but I sure felt like it.

My next partner was an older woman, maybe forty or fifty, wearing ear-rings, a blue blouse and a bright red skirt. I'd seen her before and she was a fine dancer. When she'd go around she'd lay her head back and her hair would swing out. She had some fancy kicking steps too.

"Boyka," (boy) she said when she asked me to dance. "Lempi says I give you more lesson, eh?" At first I felt as though I were dancing with my mother but that soon passed. I don't know how she managed it, probably by leading me, but soon I was really having a fine old time. Exhilarating! I was disappointed when the number ended and she refused to dance again with me. "No, boyka, that's 'nough teaching. I like polka too much." With a motherly bit of affection she touched my cheek as I left her.

By this time I'd gotten up enough nerve to ask some of the other girls to dance. One of them turned me down. "You not too good dancer for me," she said haughtily but the girl beside her offered to take her place and off we went. Altogether I think I must have danced with nine different girls before the evening ended. Some of the dances were disasters and we just couldn't fit together but others went fine.

One of the best of them was the one with Olga Pukkinen, the youngest of the girls with the green ribbons in their hair. She sure held me tight but when she asked me if I had the green ribbon and I said no, she seemed to lose interest and wouldn't dance with me again.

I think it was about eleven thirty when the first real trouble began. It was getting very hot up there in the loft and a big Finn started to pry open the big door at one end of the room, the one through which hay had formerly been brought in. "No!" yelled Mrs. Pukkinen. "No open door. Leave be! You hot, go outside or drink red pop here. Ten cents." She pointed to the washtub full of ice chunks and pop bottles.

The big Finn pretended he didn't hear her and began kicking the door to loosen it. When Mrs. Pukkinen ran over and grabbed him he flung her off contemptuously. "Eino!" she then yelled. "Eino, tulleh, tulleh" (Come, come!). Up the stairs came her big son and as his mother held the Finn's arms, Eino slugged him in the jaw. It was quite evident that they'd had practiced it before. Anyway, it was all over in a minute and we could hear the big Finn's head bumping on the stairsteps as Eino dragged the limp body outside. Mrs. Pukkinen opened herself a bottle of red pop. "Moosik! More moosik now!" she commanded and the ball went on.

There were two or three more bits of trouble as the crowd got liquored up. The old lady would not permit any drinking up in the loft except for her red pop. When one of the men tilted a bottle and offered to pass it around, she grabbed him by the collar and seat of the pants and threw him downstairs. Didn't even have to call for Eino that time. Did it by herself. Also there were several arguments that got louder and louder with blows being threatened. Mrs. Pukkinen stopped them by yelling, "You no fight here. You want fight, go outside!" They did and some of us went down the stairs to watch, to get some fresh air and to take a leak. Not very good fights; all roundhouse slugging that ended when by chance a blow connected. And no bad feelings either. The winners bought the losers a shot of Eino's moonshine and that ended the matter. Powerful stuff, that moonshine, Mullu said.

The only dangerous melee began when one of the men began badgering the drummer. Pretty well tanked up, he kept trying to bang the bass drum with his red pop bottle and it spoiled the beat of the music. The drummer, a little man, bore the nuisance as well as he could for a time but when his annoyer began using his bald head for a drumskin, he pulled out a long knife and went for the pest. Fortunately, others stepped in, took away the knife, and threw the man out. Then when he came back in again, the old lady called for Eino who came up, did his duty, and the band played on!

By midnight, most of the dancers had begun to pair up. Often a couple would leave the loft for a time, returning a bit flushed and ready for more red pop. I noticed that the Pukkinen girls especially were doing that often, first with one man, then with another, and then another.

But it wasn't until I heard old lady Pukkinen shout that I knew what was happening. "Aili! Aili" she yelled "If he aint got the green ribbon, don't you give it!"

Quite an evening!

THE SECRET PLACE

It was August the first, the day after his sixth birthday, and the boy was sure feeling good. For breakfast he'd had a bowl of fresh blueberries, two pancakes with thick home-made maple syrup, three brown sausage sticks, and one long hug from his mother. Leaving the kitchen, the boy sat for a bit on the back steps, letting the sunshine tingle the skin under his shirt. "What'll I do today?" he asked himself with anticipation.

His mother provided the first answer. "Cully," she said. "Remember that you're six years old now and have chores to do. It's baking day and I need some kindling and firewood." The boy felt big as he went out to the barn. Yes, he was six years old now and would be in the first grade when school started again. No more being called "Kindergarten baby, slopped in the gravy" by the big kids. No sir! He was getting to be a big kid himself. Proud to have chores to do, the boy so overloaded his arms with the kindling that many pieces fell off on the way back to the house thereby requiring two more trips. Then, when he returned for the firewood, he discovered that five sticks, then four sticks, and even three sticks were too heavy so he brought the wood in two at a time. After three more trips, his arms were tired so he went into the chicken yard to gather the eggs. That was chore number two.

The boy was always a little scared when he opened the chicken yard gate because that old rooster had chased him once, but this time it was busy scratching in a corner. "Phew!" the boy said as he entered the shed, his nose wrinkling from the smell of the rows of white manure under the roosts. Only two brown eggs were in the upper nesting boxes but a big hen sat clucking in a lower one. Probably the broody hen that his father had been hanging in a burlap bag the week before. Gingerly the boy tried to feel around under her only to get a sharp peck that sent him fleeing. It hurt! Angry, and forgetting the eggs, he'd gone to collect, the boy chased the other chickens in the yard until they squawked even though he well knew better. Mean old biddy! Maybe his father would chop off her head and they'd have her for dinner next Sunday.

The boy also forgot chore number three which was to sweep the front porch. Instead he walked down the board sidewalk to the Beltaire's house, being careful not to step on a crack. "Step on a crack and break your mother's back" - that was the old saying. When Mrs. Beltaire came to the door and he asked if Rudy could come out to play, she said no, that Rudy and the rest of the family were out picking berries and wouldn't be back till supper time.

That was too bad. Rudy and he had been building an iron mine in his sand pile the day before. They'd dug the shaft and used the dirt for the ore piles. Rudy was going to bring a couple of the little wooden boxes that dried codfish came in; they could serve both as tram cars and the skip that hauled the iron ore out of the hole. The boy dug the shaft a bit deeper, made some railroad tracks leading to the mine, then suddenly remembered the huge pipes that they used to get the water out. His father had taken him for a tour of the mine once and, although he'd been fascinated by the flapping belts of the big steam engine and the wheels turning around on top of the shaft, one of the most interesting things was watching the heavy flow of water coming out of those big pipes. It even made a creek that flowed into Fish Lake, his father had said. Yes, the boy thought, he had to get some pipes for his play mine.

He found some steel ones after considerable hunting but they were too long and big so he tried rolling up some tubes of newspaper. No good! They kept unrolling. Then he remembered seeing some of those big weed canes he and Rudy had once used for blow guns. They were hollow and just about the right size. Oh yes, there was a patch of them at the edge of the grove. As he crossed the street and entered the woods the boy noticed that he had been saying to himself over and over again: "North pole and south pole and south pole and north pole." Kind of a chant, it was, so he began to say it aloud. "North Pole and South Pole, and South Pole and North Pole." Didn't make any sense.

The boy never found those weed canes for his mine pipes, but he did find patches of violets, not just the blue ones but some big yellow ones and a few little white ones too. They kept falling out of one hand as he picked with the other but he was able to keep enough to make his mother smile when he brought them to her. That smile and her hug were almost as good as the piecrust tart sprinkled with brown sugar she gave him. He'd been hungry, doing all that work.

Which reminded him to get the eggs and sweep the porch without being asked. He even looked in the woodbox to see if he should bring in more firewood but it was full. "North Pole and South Pole." The boy tried to drown the phrase out of his mind by getting a hard stick and holding it against the picket fence as he ran beside it. It made a nice noise that became a flutter if he ran fast enough but "North Pole and South Pole" still kept echoing in his head. Hopping and skipping alternately, he made his way to Sliding Rock, a large stone outcropping on the road past Mr. Salo's place. Hundreds of children over the years had worn out their breeches on that rock. It really wasn't too tall but you slid fast and fetched up at the bottom with a good jolt to the legs.

Tiring of sliding, the boy spent some time in one of his Secret Places. He had three of them but liked this one best. It was under a huge maple tree with a thick ring of elderberry bushes around most of it but from it the boy could see almost all of our hill street and the valley below. Sure made him feel big to see the roofs of the houses far below him. He felt as though he were king of the castle and you're a dirty rascal. A black crow flew over, cawing, and the boy wished he were a bird. "I'd fly all over town," he thought, "Even over Lake Tioga or to the North Pole and the South Pole. And then I'd come back." A train whistled at the depot. He could see its white plumes of smoke and hear the clickety clack of the wheels as it gained speed. "When I'm big," he said aloud, "I'll take the train and go to... go to..." but he didn't really know where he'd want to go to.

Remembering that he'd hidden an Indian head copper penny between the roots of the big tree, he finally found it but not before he'd put a hand on a toad. "Oh, oh, now I'll get a wart," he said. "Toads make warts, and they have to be burned off." He made a beeline for the house where he washed his hands hard with soap and hot water. His mother praised him for doing so. "It is time for dinner," she said. "Your father phoned to say he wouldn't be back until much later, so you'll have to be my head of the house," and she had him sit in his father's place at the table to do the serving. Sure made him feel proud.

After dinner was over, the boy felt sleepy but he wasn't going to take a nap. No sir! He'd won that battle with his mother long before. He was six years old now. All his chores were done, so he'd just go outdoors and play. Besides, if he stayed inside to look at picture books he might fall asleep. No, he'd make himself an Indian war bonnet, using the feather he'd seen in the chicken yard that morning. "North Pole and South Pole." He found the feather and some string. Not too hard tying the feather to the string but when he attempted to make a loop that would fit his head the boy had a miserable time. Finally, he threw it on the ground, spit on it, and ground it under his foot. "I don't want to play Indian anyway," he said.

No, he'd be a cowboy soldier and fight the Indians. Two sticks were all he needed to make an imaginary sword and horse and he galloped all over the yard beheading redskins. What he really needed though was a fort. Indians could sneak up on you when you were asleep and shoot their arrows into your heart, they could. So the boy made himself a fort in the corner of the yard by the big birch tree. He made it out of some cardboard and old packing cases, parked his imaginary horse outside it, and lay down to sleep with his trusty sword beside him. He didn't get to sleep though because a big Indian in the form of Mr. Marchand, our mail carrier, drove up the street with his team and buckboard. Instantly changing his sword into a gun, the boy shot at Indian Marchand ten times. Didn't seem to hit him or his horse but at least they went away. That was enough playing fort. "North Pole and South Pole."

He spied a bed of nasturtiums in full flower. Picking them one after another, he nipped off the long part with his teeth, then tried to suck out the honey. Yes, it was kind of sweet but not really satisfying. He found some soursap weeds and chewed them. They were sour for sure, but not like rhubarb. Rhubarb was really sour unless you put sugar on it. Or was it salt? He went to the kitchen to wrap a bit of both in pieces of newspaper, then dipped a stalk of rhubarb first in one, then in the other. Both were so sour they screwed up his mouth. The boy shook his head. "Raspberry tucks are good with salt," he said aloud to himself. He peeled the outer layer from some new shoots, dipped them in the salt, and nibbled. "Not as good as in spring," he said. They were tougher than he had remembered. "North Pole and South Pole."

About three thirty, he returned to the house for a cookie and a cup of milk. "What have you been doing all day, Cully?" asked his mother. "Nothing," he answered. "Just playing. Is it all right if I go to see Uncle Timmy and Aunt Kathleen?" She agreed.

The O'Brians were no relatives but they liked kids so much, having none of their own, that all of us called them Aunt and Uncle. The boy was one of their favorites. Uncle Timmy could hold up a silver dollar in his hand, then suddenly make it disappear. He also could take his teeth right out of his mouth if you said the magic word. Anybody could do it, Uncle Timmy claimed. When you asked what that magic word was, he'd tell you but he said it so fast it was hard to remember. It was something like "allegazoofamatachang" but the boy had never been able to get it right and so, no matter how he tugged, his teeth stayed in his mouth. The O'Brian house was always full of laughter and Aunt Kathleen made the best gingerbread in town.

But on his way over there, the boy suddenly decided to go to Africa instead after seeing an ant lion emerge from its hole in a ring of sand, then duck back in again. The little bug wasn't a real lion, of course, but that was its name and the kids said that like real lions you had to hit it in the eye with a spear if you wanted to kill it. That meant that the boy had to make a spear but by the time he had found a likely poplar shoot that could serve as one he'd forgotten all about Africa and lions.

Instead he spent a long time putting up a little shack of fallen branches at his second Secret Place. He built it over his special Mossy Stone, the one covered with soft green fuzz on which he had often sat. It would be his deer hunting cabin, just like the one his father had in the forest. Moving the branches to make a porthole, he aimed a pretend gun and shot ten deer, one after another. Big ones too, with horns like the one that hung in his father's den. Then, needing to urinate, he held off until he could scrape away some leaves to make an outhouse. Instead of unbuttoning the fly of his pants, the boy just let them fall down to his knees, his hips being barely able to hold them up anyway. By arching and moving the stream, he put out a forest fire even bigger than the one that had scared the whole town the summer before.

As the boy pulled up his pants, he saw his navel. The other kids called it a belly button but his mother always said 'navel.' When he'd asked her about it, pointing out that there wasn't any button at all, she'd explained. "No, there's no button, Cully," she had said. "Before you were being born, you lived in my tummy until you got big enough to be a baby. And even after you came out, you were fastened to me by a stem, like the stem of an apple is fastened to its tree. Your navel is just what's left of the stem that joined you and me." The boy shook his head; he never had quite understood it, and still didn't. He sure felt tired and sleepy and sick of saying "North Pole and South Pole and South Pole and North Pole" so, to stop it, he put up two sticks on opposite sides of his brush shack. "You're the North Pole," he said to the first, and "You're the South Pole," he said to the second, "So now shut up!" He sure was tired.

When the boy had not returned by five o'clock, his mother went to the O'Brians. No, Cully hadn't shown up there at all, they told her. They'd seen him going into the grove that morning though. No, mother said, he'd been home for dinner and had asked her if it was OK to visit them. That had been about three or four o'clock. Tim O'Brian offered to walk uptown to Flinn's store, asking people if anyone had seen the boy, and did so even when the boy's mother had said no. She called his name over and over again down by the grove, then again by Sliding Rock, and the school yard. She walked over to Swedetown calling and asking. By six o'clock she was so frantic the boy's father could scarcely understand what she was telling him. There had been bears around town that had made way with a hog or two. A six year old boy wasn't very big. The thought was unbearable.

His mother was sitting on the porch wringing her hands when the boy crawled out from under it. That was his third Secret Place and he'd been sleeping in it on leaves and a burlap sack.

THE CONVERT

When Tioga was in its prime with five mines working full blast, and the great white pine forest was being slaughtered, our village had five churches. The Catholic church whose bells filled the valley with their ringing was furthest down our hill street. Next came the Finnish Lutheran with its tall, narrow and pointed windows. Opposite old Blue Ball's house was the Methodist Episcopal church which we attended and back of it on a little side street was the Swedish Lutheran. Also, southeast of the mine there stood a little wooden church with tall pillars by its portico that ran up twenty feet to the roof and on that roof was a steeple that looked like a big wooden tulip bulb. Long abandoned by the time I was a boy, it had been the church of the Slavs who had worked in the mines. People think of New York City as the melting pot of America but when the mines were going strong we had our own melting pot right in our own village.

Generally, our people were a god-fearing, god-loving lot, even when they were sinners of a sort. No big sins, just a lot of little ones and they went to church more for companionship than from hell fear. More women attended regularly than did our men mainly because the latter worked hard six days a week and the Sabbath had to be saved for rest, fishing and poaching. However, every man had one good suit, his marriage-burial suit that he could wear when he did attend. He never felt particularly comfortable in it but he'd have felt more uneasy in his stagged pants or overalls. Shoes were worse yet and many arguments occurred about his having to wear them to church with the good suit. Maybe that's why more women attended than men.

The biggest congregation belonged to the Catholics. Their church was always filled on Sundays which was more than one could say for the Protestants. There were several reasons for this. First of all, it was a beautiful little church because a large stained south window behind the high altar filled the place with color. The statuary in the niches of the seven stations of the cross, together with the many tall candles lit by the acolytes at the beginning of the service, helped give the impression that it was indeed a holy place. In many ways ours was a rather barren land and to its parishioners the Catholic church provided not only mysticism but beauty.

Secondly, it gave the French Canadians a special feeling of heritage. The ancient rituals, the Latin masses, were the same ones their ancestors had known in France. When you were in church you were glad you were French, glad enough to be willing to forego any meat but fish on Friday, proud to wear the grey mark on your forehead on Ash Wednesday. It was good to make the responses you had learned as a child in catechism school.

But the main reason that Catholics filled the church even when the snow was up to their shoulders was their priest. Father Hassel was a remarkable man. Highly educated (he could speak French and German as fluently as he could English), he was essentially a plain man of the people, able to share their feelings and concerns without the slightest condescension. He wasn't stuck up at all, the people said. A short man, with a big resonant voice, he dominated every gathering, yet Father Hassel's joviality and wit and ready laugh always put you at ease. All the people in town liked and respected him, even the Finns. We saw him often for he was always out tending all his flock, not just the sick or dying, and when we met him we called him Father just as the Catholics did. They said he never begged or threatened, as other priests had done, when the church needed money. He didn't have to. They gave all that they could, knowing that he would give it to poor people in trouble.

There were a lot of good stories about Father Hassel's sense of humor, some of them true. One, that may not have been true, claimed that once in the middle of a Latin prayer, not the Mass, he noticed that the altar boy hadn't brought the incense. Without breaking his cadence, Father Hassel chanted "Where the hell is the incense pot?" to which the acolyte intoned in the same fashion "Dropped it in the aisle; it was too damned hot." Nobody in the congregation batted an eye.

But Father Hassel could be tough too, as witness the penance he gave Paddy Feeny, our blacksmith, when he and the others put Dinny Calahan in the coffin after he'd passed out from too much booze, and then held an Irish wake over him. "You'll clean and mow and take care of the cemetery for two years, my son," he roared. And Paddy did.

The Protestant preachers rarely stayed long enough to build the relationships that Father Hassel had. Each of them not only had to serve sinners of Tioga but also those in two other towns in the area. They had to do some real humping each weekend to get to all of them, often having to shag a ride in the caboose of a freight train when the passenger train schedules were unsuitable. A preacher might hold services in one town Saturday evening, catch the train for Tioga next morning, then find some way to get to the third town after supper. You must remember that at that time our roads between towns were at best only wagon ruts that became almost impassable even for a horse and buggy if it so much as rained. Although Father Hassel was pleasantly plump we never had a fat Protestant minister.

The Finnish Luthern church just up the hill from the Catholic church had thirty nine steps leading up to it from our street but the faithful always climbed them willingly. Services were always conducted in the Finnish language, the men and boys sitting on one side of the corner aisle with the women, in their head shawls, and the girls on the other. Their hymns, in a minor key, sounded pretty mournful but that church had the sweetest sounding bells in Tioga. Even without looking closely we could know if a couple on their way to church were Finns or not. The man always led the way down the sidewalk with the woman following.

Our own church, the Methodist Episcopal, didn't have a cross or a steeple, but it did have a choir loft big enough to hold Aunt Lizzie and five or six other singers. It's pews were the most uncomfortable in town and they were painted with a varnish that always clung to your pants when you had to rise. It was a plain Jane of a church with a lectern-pulpit instead of an altar and its two big pot bellied stoves never seemed to heat it well enough to keep you from seeing your breath in the winter. Our congregations were small but they could sure belt out the old familiar hymns. Comparatively liberal, it was the one church where itinerant evangelists could hold old time revival meetings full of hell and damnation.

I don't know much about the Swedish Luthern church because I never attended any service there. It was said to be very bare in the Scandinavian fashion. Certainly it was very strict in its teachings. Swede kids couldn't go out to play on Sunday afternoons but stayed inside their homes reading the bible or something. There weren't very many of them after the mines closed and the white pine was gone.

You might think that this situation meant trouble, that each denomination would try to raid other congregations to make converts but that had not happened. For one thing Father Hassel was too busy keeping track of the members of his parish who hadn't been to confession regularly; for another, the Protestant preachers just didn't have the time or energy. Besides, the people in our village had long learned to live together with some peace; they liked things the way they were.

There was, however, one person in Tioga who did his damndest to convert others to his irreligious point of view. His name was Erkki Tuppinen and the Finns had a word for him that meant trouble-maker. A small man, barely five feet, three inches tall but very strong, he had been a miner until he was kicked out of town when he tried to organize a union. Henry Thompson, the tough mine superintendent, had personally put him aboard a through freight to Chicago with only one hour's notice. "We don't want any radicals here!" he roared. "You come back and you'll leave again but in a pine box."

Thompson had been right. Erkki was a true radical, proudly dubbing himself both an atheist and an anarchist. He was that way when he left, and that way when he returned twenty years later, only more so. He was smart too and studied a lot of books so he was tough to argue with. If you listened to him long enough, you almost began to think he might have a point in his railings. Most of us didn't listen; we just let him spout off and went our way. He was too small to hit.

Erkki said the most outrageous things and of course they traveled up and down our hill street and all over the valley. When he questioned the virginity of the Virgin Mary when talking to our weather prophet, Sieur Rosseau, it was all the Prophet could do to keep from squashing him through the knothole in the post office floor. Erkki told the Swedish Luthern minister face to face that God was a bad dream dreamed by an idiot. Erkki read the bible more, and went to church, not only the Finnish Luthern but all of the others, more than any man in town - but only to gather ammunition for his arguments. Where he got the passages he could quote from the bible, I don't know but he sure could pick the ones that put God in a bad light.

As an anarchist Erkki was equally obnoxious. He insisted that all government was evil, that we'd be a lot better without a president, a governor, or Dr. Gage, my father, the township supervisor. He said all they did was to take away money from the poor workers and give it to the rich. "You're all blind slaves," he said. Yes, he was a radical all right, but as a persuader he didn't amount to much. If he ever managed to get one convert, I don't know who it was. He sure tried, year after year, but our people never got the message.

I said earlier that none of our church members tried to do any missionary work within the village but that isn't quite right. A small band of Finns, dissatisfied with the teachings of their church, broke away and formed a little church of their own. We called them the Holy Jumpers because of their frenzy when they got worked up during their services. At first, there were only a few families of them, holding their Sunday meetings in their own homes, but gradually by intensive persuasion they gained enough members to need a real church. Not having enough money to build one, the Holy Jumpers moved into the old Slav church southeast of the mine. They tore down the wooden tulip-shaped steeple, patched the broken boards of its walls, put in a stove, and they were in business.

It was a noisy business too. Unlike the quiet sedate services held in our other churches, the Holy Jumpers really let go. You could hear them all over uptown shouting hozannahs, praying, crying, singing, weeping, even dancing with heavenly joy.

Mullu and I went over there one Saturday night to see what was going on. From our position at the side of the front steps we could see everything that happened through the open front door. There were no pews inside, just a semicircle of rough benches, and the altar was just an upright section of a huge log. That's where the preacher, if there was any, stood, and did his chanting in Finnish. I say "if any" because one after another, the members sitting on the benches would come forward to the tree stump altar and start chanting or shouting. Mullu, who understood Finnish, said that many times he couldn't understand a word of it, that they were "speaking in tongues."

The service started quietly enough but soon the tempo and loudness of the voices began to increase. "They're begging God for mercy now," translated Mullu. Holding each other's hands, the semicircle of worshippers swayed back and forth. Suddenly one speaker began to chant and then to sing a strange song with a good beat and throwing his arms upward, danced down to the semicircle of worshippers, grabbed one of them and danced back with her or him to the tree stump. Suddenly the place was filled with people dancing solo, singing, yelling. Then one old man began to jump up and down, raising his arms upwards, evidently pleading with each jump. "He says he wants to go to heaven," Mullu whispered. "Raise me, Lord. Take me up in your arms! That's what he's yelling." Soon others were doing it too, and when they started coming out of the church still jumping and shouting and dancing Mullu and I high-tailed it out of there. It wasn't really comical at all; it was just interesting. You had to respect their sincerity and admire the joyousness with which they served their Lord.

Of course, Erkki had to visit that church too but when he entered he was surprised to find that he was welcomed warmly instead of meeting the suspicion and resentment he'd encountered at the other churches. The Holy Jumpers knew that Erkki was an atheist. No matter! He had joined them and they took him in, placed him at the center of the semicircle of benches, and, as the service began, the people on each side of him smilingly took his hands in theirs. He found himself swaying back and forth together with the other worshippers as they sang and chanted. This was not the austere, forbidding atmosphere Erkki had found in the other Protestant churches. You didn't have to sit stiffly and quietly or wear a solemn face. These people were free souls, happy in their fellowship, joyously worshipping a God full of mercy and kindness, not the cruel one he'd scoffed at so many times.

Fearful at first that he might be grabbed and forced to go up to the stump altar and say something, Erkki tried to think of some shockingly sacreligious things to say but they didn't come to him, nor did anyone try to get him to come forth. Instead, after the service was over, several people invited Erkki to come to their homes for coffee and korpua. He was too shaken to accept, but the next weekend he was back in the Holy Jumper church again. And the next and the next.

Sometime later my father and Father Hassel were having their weekly chess game in our living room. I'd brought up the whiskey and the undertaker's gift cigars from the ledge in the cellarway but of course had to clear out because it was understood by all that no one was to listen to their conversation. Perhaps because of that prohibition I crept up the back stairs, carefully avoiding that third step from the top which always shrieked when you stepped on it, then went to the bedroom above the living room. There was a round register there through which the stovepipe went to the chimney and by putting my ear on the grating I could hear everything they said.

Most of it was chess talk all about gambits and pawns and checks and checkmates but occasionally there were more interesting bits of conversation.

"Father," said Dad after a long silence, "What are the dynamics of conversion? What happens in a confirmed sinner when he suddenly sees the light and becomes a Christian?"

The priest laughed. "Ah, there you go again, Doctor, practicing psychological warfare, trying to keep me from seeing that you're sneakily planning for a checkmate by moving that bishop here and your knight there. But you do not distract me, sir, as witness this countering move."

"No, Father, I'd really like to know."

The priest was still suspicious. "Are you thinking about joining us, Doctor? Certainly it's about time you gave up that fake agnosticism of yours." He laughed again. "I'll be delighted to give you religious instructions after your office hours any time you wish. Now why are you moving your king's knight there?"

Dad was insistent. "I don't know why you won't answer my questions, father," he said. "I have a patient who's suddenly got religion. Perhaps you know him - Erkki Tuppinen, our town's atheist?"

"Sure I know him well. A few years ago he pestered me a lot, wanting to argue religion, yes, trying to convert me to atheism of all things." The priest grinned, remembering. "You mean he's joined the Finnish Lutheran church?"

"Oh no," Dad answered. "He's become a Holy Jumper and rabid one. Why even when he was in considerable pain yesterday he was intent on saving my bloody soul."

"What's ailing him, Doctor?"

"I'm not sure I have the story straight, Father," Dad answered. "From what the Kangases told me, (They're taking care of him), it seems that suddenly he joined their frenzy, began chanting and dancing and talking in tongues, and then tried to climb up one of the tall pillars in front of the door. Kept yelling that he was going to heaven and for others to follow him."

"Did he get there, Doctor?" The priest was amused.

"No, after several tries he almost got to the top but then fell and fractured both legs. Nasty fractures, they were. Hard to set right. Took me two hours before I had them in casts."

"I should think that experience would have shaken his newly found faith," Father Hassel said.

"Not at all," Dad replied. "Erkki claims he could feel Saatana, the devil, pulling down on his legs. He's sure no atheist now. Tell me, father, do you think the conversion will last? I can't believe that it could."

"Yes, I think it could," said the priest. "After all there was St. Paul on the road to Damascus. Once you've seen the glory, Doctor, you are changed forever."

The priest was right and Dad was wrong. For the rest of his days Erkki traveled the whole U.P. and northern Wisconsin, preaching his gospel and organizing new Holy Jumper churches wherever he went.

I BETCHA

Except for "Paaiva," "Bonjour" or "Good Morning" few phrases were heard as often in Tioga as the words "I betcha." With no entertainment available except that which we could contrive ourselves, we spiced up our games and activities with "I betchas." There were two kinds of "I betchas," the first being a challenge and the second a true wager. When a new kid came to town the first thing he heard was "I betcha I kin lick you!" We didn't need any wood chip on the shoulder to start a good fight. Similarly, when someone said to me, "Cully, I betcha can't climb the front face of Mount Baldy" I had to make the attempt, thereby contracting a fear of heights that has never left me. Clinging to that crevice with my fingernails, unable to see any way to go up or down that sheer cliff, the experience is as shudderingly vivid now as it was then, seventy years ago.

In the U.P., courage has always been viewed as a necessary trait and in that rough land at the turn of this century I guess it was. To feel that you were cowardly was unbearable. By example and precept our fathers and our peers made it very clear that challenges were to be accepted no matter what the consequences. The result was that all of us boys did a lot of foolhardy things. We swam in the ring of lake water surrounding the big ice cake every spring. We dared each other to tip-toe across the wet stringers of the railroad bridge. We crawled under the barbed wire that was supposed to keep us out of old mine pits and precariously made our way down the steep slopes to the dark water beneath them. We ran across the pasture where we knew Salo's big bull would chase us. All of these foolhardy adventures started with some kid saying, "I betcha!" How we ever made it to adulthood I don't know.

The other kind of "I betchas" had to do with real betting, though only rarely was any money involved. We didn't have any! Or, if we'd managed to earn a nickel spending three hours hoeing quack grass out of the potato patch, that was too precious to risk in a wager. Why, for a nickel you could buy a lot of candy - a jaw breaker, a stick of licorice, a bit of horehound and a gum drop. No, instead of money we used marbles, hazelnuts, wads of chewed spruce gum and matches or other valuables. You might wonder that matches had enough value to serve as the currency of our betting but back then they really did. One match was used to light the stove or campfire but after that our men lit their corncob pipes with spills, very thin shavings of cedar, that flared immediately when touched to the flame. Every housewife hoped to have a few live coals in the morning ashes of her kitchen range so that she wouldn't have to waste a match. When we swiped matches from the pantry to use on our expeditions or in our shacks, we never dared take a handful but only two or three at most because they wouldn't be noticed.

Marbles of course were always valuable because we played with them all year long, yes, at times even in the winter if the temperature had managed to get up to ten below. The kind of marbles we played was totally different from the squat down, knuckle flicking game that kids from outside the U.P. played. That was sissy stuff. We cleared a ring in the snow or dirt, packed it down and smoothed its surface, then "dobbed in." Dobbing in meant that a large marble, the "fats," was placed in the center of the ring and each boy put his marble at some spot within its circumference. Then we took turns flinging our "shooters" at the fats from a distance of ten or twelve feet. If your shooter hit the fats, you got all the marbles in the ring. If you missed, you had to dob in another marble and the next kid got his turn. If you hit another boys' marble it was yours. It was marksmanship and luck and a lot of mathematics too because different kinds of marbles had different values. The "commy," a dull clay marble, had the least value. A "crockery" was worth five commies; a "glassy," seven commies; a "cats-eye" eight; a "steelie," which was a ball bearing, was worth ten. A common agate could bring you fifteen commies or three crockeries in trade; but a "blood agate," the most valuable of them all, was worth one hundred commies.

We always started by dobbing in commies but soon the ring got so crowded with them, we made it tougher on the next shooter by substituting marbles of higher value. For example, if there were thirty five commies, three steelies, and three common agates in the right, you could take them all out by putting one blood agate in their place. That left only two targets, the fats and the blood agate instead of forty-one. I know it sounds complicated and it was. Took a lot of adding, subtracting, multiplying, and usually a lot of arguing, but it was fun. Some games could last for many hours before one of us had all the marbles in our breeches. Anyway, you can see why marbles were our wampum.

We also gambled with those marbles when playing cards - usually in Mullu's barn. He had an old deck of greasy sticky cards that we'd have to dust with flour before trying to shuffle them. For games like smear or mustamaya (hearts) each player would put marbles in the pot with winner take all. But draw poker was our favorite and all of us were playing it before we were nine years old. No deuces wild for us; we played the old classic game, betting our marbles after each draw with the cards held close to our chests and blankness on our faces. Somehow I never learned how to bluff at the right time, so I usually lost. Once, the crew cleaned me out of every marble I had in my pockets, even my one treasured blood agate.

Occasionally we also played nosey poker in much the same fashion except that you put the marbles you bet in front of you rather than in the pot. Then, after all the betting was done, the winner not only took losers' marbles but also could sideswipe their noses with a card held by one corner, once for each marble they had lost. While it wasn't fair to hit the nose with the edge of the card, it still stung plenty. Rosy-nosey was what we called that game. It sure taught us how to bet conservatively.

We didn't confine our gambling to cards however, and we didn't always use marbles or matches in our betting. For example, when my mother looked out of the bay window and saw me coming home from school one noon on all fours with a bunch of kids enjoying the spectacle, she couldn't understand what had happened to me. It was simple. I'd made the mistake of betting Mullu I could stand on one leg longer than he could. We called that kind of gambling "Loser Pays."

Once Mule Cardinal, Reino, Iggy and I were spending the night in my father's hunting cabin. We'd carried up half a bushel of potatoes to go with the fish we caught and had cooked most of them in a big kettle. After we were gorged, Iggy bet Mule that he would kiss his naked butt if he could eat all the potatoes that were left. Lord, the kettle was still half full of them and it took Mule some time before accepting the wager. Potato after potato went down his gullet. Mule took down his pants. "Only four more to go, Iggy!" he said. Three more, two more. Mule never could eat that last one. With his eyeballs popping and holding his stomach, he crawled groaning into the lower bunk and never moved till morning. All of us except Iggy were disappointed.

Just one more example of Loser Pays. Four of us were fishing trout in Wolf Creek, this time with a vengeance, because we'd agreed that the one who caught the fewest would have to kiss Phyllis DuChame. We started out at the same time and were to meet at the bridge at five o'clock. Trout had to be seven inches or better. You might think that the loser in this case would be the winner but if so, you didn't know Phyllis. She was pretty enough but she was a wildcat. Any boy who tried to kiss her would not just get his face slapped; he'd have it clawed. Well Fisheye lost that one because he only had seven trout on his stringer at five o'clock. At five o'clock the next day Fisheye also had seven deep scratches on his mug. Loser pays!

We also had another gambling game in Tioga called Take-the-Last-One. We would each put an equal number of marbles or matches in the pot for winner take all, or set up some Loser-pays kind of wager. Usually only two kids played this game, but more could if so desired. The object was, after a series of drawings, to take the last marble or match. Thus, if there were ten matches in the pot, and we could choose either one or two matches when it was our turn to draw, the number in the pot would gradually decrease until they were all gone, the winner being the kid who drew the last match.

It was my beloved Grampa Gage who taught me how to win every time. No, he didn't give me the magic formula; he let me discover it myself. That formula is this: draw so that the number of remaining matches is a multiple of the number of choices plus one. Thus if you can choose either one or two matches when you have your turn, the magic number is two plus one (three), thus you draw from the ten marble pot so that what's left are nine, six or three. Once the pot gets down to three, if your opponent takes one, you take two; if he takes two, you take one. Either way, you take the last one and win. The game can be played with any number of marbles in the pot or any number of choices but so long as you draw so that the remaining matches are a multiple of choices plus one, you can't possibly lose. Try it and you'll see. I made a lot of pocket money in college trimming suckers with Take-the-Last-One. Grandpa Gage also gave me some good advice. "Let them win enough times to keep them playing," he said.

You might think that all of this betting would have led to addiction in later years but to my knowledge there was only one man in Tioga who could be called a compulsive gambler. His name was Jim Fortas. A gaunt scarecrow of a man, he had a good job in the round house back of the depot, greasing, oiling and doing maintenance on the locomotives there. Every monthly payday Jim took his paycheck of $160 up to Flinn's store, bought five loaves of bread, three bags of korpua, a slab of bacon, a ham, coffee and ten cans of pork and beans. Then he took his change entirely in silver dollars, half dollars, quarters and dimes, his betting money for the next month. People said it was a good thing he'd never married because he usually lost it all before the next paycheck came due, and had to eat pretty low on the hog those last days.

So far as we knew Jim Fortas had never shown any interest in women. His first and last love was gambling. He'd bet with anyone on anything, but he preferred creating pools. He'd bring around a sheet entitled "When will the ice break up in Lake Tioga?", let you pick any date and time you wished, and sign your name, and then he'd collect your dollar. Jim was absolutely honest so we trusted him with the money but just to make sure he always gave it to Charley Olafson to hold and the sheet was posted on the bulletin board at the town hall. Jim organized such betting pools on when the first maple sap would run, on how deep the snow would get, on the highest temperature in summer and the lowest in winter among other things. Never did Jim ever win one of his pools but once he came close, and that kept him going.

People said Jim was a good loser and he was. All he ever said when he lost a bet was "OK, next time!" We didn't know what he said when he won because that happened so rarely. Jim was one of the regulars down at the Saturday night poker sessions in the back room of Callahan's store and was always greeted by "Welcome, sucker!" when he appeared.

To Jim a day without a wager was a lost day. He didn't lose many of them. Even on Sunday, he'd be there at church door trying to make a bet on how long the sermon would last or on how many Amens Mrs. O'Connor would yelp. He'd be in the post office trying to get a bet on the weather or the temperature for the following day or night. At Higley's Saloon Jim nursed a beer until he could find someone who would bet on how soon Joe Kroops would fall off his stool. In the depot, he made bets on how late the evening South Shore train would be. Everyone was glad to oblige Jim when he said "I betcha" because he was almost sure to lose.

Oh there were times, I'm sure, when his consistent losing must have got to him, and, as he told the story, he'd once studied the behavior of the swallows that sat in a row on the telephone wires. For many days he watched those birds trying to discover which one would leave the wire first. It was always the one at the end of the row. But which end? It was the bird that the wind hit first. Over and over again, that was the first bird to leave the wire. So Jim bet five dollars with Pete Lacosse that he could pick the first bird to leave when seventeen swallows were perching there on the wire. That looked like pretty good odds to Pete so he plunked down his five bucks. What happened? A bird in the middle of the row was the first to fly off.

Our people began to be ashamed of always taking Jim's money and they tried hard to get him to quit gambling. Our minister had a long talk with him. His friends at the round house tried too. One of them even made a two dollar bet with him that he couldn't stop betting for two days in a row. Jim paid off, saying he'd quit for one day and that was enough, that a man needed a little excitement as much or more than he needed meat.

Nevertheless, there came a time when Jim Fortas overcame his addiction. Pete Ramos presented him with the left front foot of a rabbit that had been shot at midnight as a good luck charm. "You have to keep that rabbit foot in your left hand hind pocket and stroke it just before you make a bet," he said. "Stroke it three times, no more."

Well, Jim thought that was all nonsense but hell he had nothing to lose so he gave it a try. And he won! Then he made another bet and won again. What's more, day after day he kept winning every bet he made. Oh, Jim knew that Lady Luck was an erratic goddess and, having been so unlucky so long, it was only fitting that at last he was having a winning streak. Surely, it couldn't last. But it did. Often he made a bet that he was certain he would lose but still he won. A crazy business.

Gambling wasn't much fun any more. Every time Jim did lose, which was seldom, he could feel the old excitement but that soon passed when he won again. Finally he took that rabbits leg and heaved it into the swamp. Still he kept winning. Down at Callahan's store on Saturday night, he'd bet a pile when all he held were two threes and the others would fold and let him have the pot. Once when Dinny Callahan laid down three kings, Jim filled an inside straight. Once, for the first time in his life, he got a royal flush. People began to shy away when Jim said "I betcha," so he started offering odds so attractive they were absurd. Again he won. At the end of the month he had lots of money. What the hell, Bill! His whole life style had been wrecked. No point to gambling if you can't lose.

So Jim Fortas quit gambling and got married, the biggest gamble of all.

EASTER

ld Man McGee hadn't slept at all well. Three times that night he had gotten out of bed to light a match so he could tell what time it was because this year he was damned if he was going to miss the sunrise service again. His old bones, groaning

as he got out of the bunk, told him he didn't have many more Easters coming to him. "Yes, McGee," he said aloud, "this time you're not a-lying in them blankets when they're singing and praying on the hill and a-yelling Hallelujah as the sun comes up. No siree, McGee!"

The old man lit the kerosene lamp and the kindling in the stove, then, holding his big stem-winder watch in his hand, crawled back under the covers to calm his shivers. When he looked at the watch again it said four thirty and the windows of his cabin were gray with new light. "Up you go, McGee!" he commanded himself, creakingly getting out of the bed, "Daylight in the swamp!" There was no time to cook coffee after he put on his Sunday suit so he fortified himself with first one finger, then two, from the brown bottle on the shelf. The whiskey warmed him but it didn't seem quite right to start Easter that way so he made amends by reading a bit from the bible that lay open on the table.

"And very early they went to the tomb when the sun had risen. And they were saying to one another, "Who will roll away the stone for us from the door of the tomb?" And looking up, they saw that the stone was rolled back; for it was very large. And, entering the tomb, they saw a young man sitting on the right side, dressed in a white robe; and they were amazed. And he said to them, "Do not be amazed; you seek Jesus of Nazareth, who was crucified. He has risen; he is not here; see the place where they laid him..."

Feeling a bit more virtuous, old man McGee put on his cap and mackinaw and started up the hill. The eastern sky had some reddish yellow in it. As he walked he kept mulling over what he had just read. Maybe the young man in the white robe was Jesus himself. Perhaps he wore the robe to cover up his wounds. Anyway the point of it was that you didn't have to stay dead if you died. That was good to know, now that the birds were singing again.

But where were the people? Usually on Easter Sunday there would at least be a few Catholics going to early Mass. Perhaps it was still too early. He pulled the watch from his pocket and put it to his ear. It was OK. Five minutes to five and the sunrise services were to begin five o'clock sharp. Maybe all the Protestants were already on the little hill by the cemetery. When he got there however, not a soul was around. What was wrong? Maybe they'd called it off because the preacher couldn't come.

Old man McGee was disappointed. He was also very tired from climbing the hill so he sat down on the mourner's bench at the edge of the cemetery to rest. What a beautiful day it was! Fresh as new mown hay. The old man breathed deeply, savoring the clean U.P. air. Now bits of sun could be seen through the tall firs on the hills, sending shafts of light across the valley where little white curls of smoke had begun to rise from the houses.

McGee was glad he'd come even though nobody else had. Still he felt lonely up there on the hilltop so he went among the grave stones looking for the names of old friends. "Mary Petry 1863-1904" Oh, he'd sure had a crush on Mary. Prettiest girl he'd ever seen. She'd let him down kindly-like when he proposed. "Good thing, too," the old man said aloud to himself. "You never amounted to much, McGee. Never could have given her what she needed..."

There were a lot of headstones that brought back memories, some bad, some good. The best were those of his old cronies, especially Jim Cronin and Arvid Aola. Lord, he'd missed those two crazy buggers for fifteen years now. The Unholy Three, they called themselves. Never a dull moment when they were together. He remembered the time when they, along with other lumberjacks from their camp, fought those from a rival camp in Shingleton for two days and nights until the town burned down. And that night up in Big Bay when the three of them cleaned out its saloon. For years they had hunted deer from the same cabin up by the Haysheds. Now only he was left.

It sure seemed a shame to have to waste that brilliant sunrise and go back down to his cabin. Suddenly, the idea came to him that he might as well conduct a sunrise service by himself. If only he had brought along his bible! No matter! He'd give it a try.

So there on the hilltop as the sun came up old man McGee celebrated the last Easter he was ever to have. He knew he wasn't doing it very well but he called all his dead friends to worship and then he sang what he could remember of the old hymn:

"Christ the Lord is risen today, Allelujah,
Sons of men and angels say, Allelujah"

What comes next? Oh, yes, the prayer. So the gaunt old Scot prayed:
"Lord," he said reverently. "I ain't much at this praying business
but I got the feeling you won't mind. I just want to ask one favor,
Lord, and that's to forgive all these friends of mine here of their sins.
And mine too. We done a lot of things we wished we hadn't but we
weren't really too bad in our hearts. "Amen!" His congregation of
tombstones shone in the morning sun.

Then the offering. McGee fumbled in his pocket for the fifty
cent piece he'd brought along and put it beside a little scrawny
dandelion, the first flower he'd seen that spring. Again he said Amen.

What comes next? Oh, the Doxology. All McGee could remember
were two lines and he wasn't sure he had them right but in his cracked
old voice he sang them anyway:

"Praise God from whom all blessings flow,
Praise God, all critters here below..."

Next would come the reading from the Bible but that was sitting
on the table down in his cabin so old man McGee extemporized. It
didn't sound very biblical but he did the best he could. "I say unto you
that they killed Jesus. Stabbed him, they did, and put his body in a
cave and rolled a big rock so he couldn't get out. But Jesus, he did get
out by pushing that rock away. And when some women looked in the
cave there he was in a white robe saying unto them," (Old man McGee
liked the sound of that unto, so he said it again), "saying unto them,
'Look! You don't have to stay dead. I am risen and you can be too.' "

Sitting on the mourner's bench, he thought about it for a while.
Then, addressing his congregation of tombstones, he added, "A man's
more than his bones, and ye know that better than McGee does..."
His voice trailed off. He knew he'd have to think up something for
the sermon so he closed his eyes. The sun, warm and tingly on his face,
made him feel drowsy.

Suddenly he heard music coming up from the valley. And
beautiful singing that grew louder and louder until he was immersed
in it. Suddenly too he found himself at the bottom but center of a great
semicircular stairs filled with cherubim and seraphim, angels and
archangels, all the heavenly host. And at the bottom rung there were
all his old friends including Jim and Arvid clad in white gowns,
playing gold harps and sprouting new wings.

"Well, if it aint Scotty McGee!" Jim and Arvid exclaimed together
as they twanged their harps. "Where the hell have you been? We've
been waiting for you?"

When old man McGee awoke, he went down the hill street meeting

Jan Peterson on the way. "Going to church, Jan?" he asked.

"Naw! Today's Saturday. I'll be going tomorrow. Where you been?"

"I've been to sunrise services," said old man McGee!

CAMPFIRES

W hen I've had trouble falling asleep I count campfires, not sheep. Actually I don't just count them; I relive them. Perhaps the measure of man's life are the campfires he has enjoyed. There's something about building a little fire at dusk in a deep forest that seems to trigger atavistic feelings the cavemen must have shared ten thousand years ago. The darkness that gradually engulfs you, then sweeps up the great trees is suddenly conquered by a tiny flame on a bit of birch bark. To watch that flame lick its way along the sticks and logs, lifting forked tongues of light until again you can see your legs and arms and body is tremendously reassuring. You are there again; you are safe. The things that go thump in the night hold no terror when you are master of the flame. Though I've built a thousand fires in my time I never fail to get some of that feeling when I put a match to tinder.

There is also something about a fire that is very healing. No one can watch a fire very long before finding a bit of the peace that passeth understanding creeping over him. Some hot summer evenings I even build a little fire on our home hearth while the air conditioner is on, so I can find my troubles fading away. Fire can burn you but it also can cleanse you. A remarkable instance of this occurred atop a high granite bluff when I was one and twenty. Two old reprobates and I had hiked all afternoon up to the headwaters of the Tioga where we'd heard there was a huge beaver dam filled with brook trout. Lars was an ex-game warden who'd been fired for poaching deer out of season among other things. Nick was an ex-convict who'd spent ten years in prison for killing a man with his fists and then stomping him in a fit of fury. Both had sinned every sin in the good book and their faces showed it. But both Lars and Nick were fine fishermen and knew the territory up there so I was glad to be along.

It was too dark to fish when we got there so, to escape the mosquitoes, we climbed to the top of a high bluff and built a fire to fry our bologna and potatoes and to cook our coffee. After they passed a bottle around and it was empty Nick and Lars started telling me about some of their dirty deeds, matching each other to see who'd done the worst, and laughing when they saw a shocked expression on my face. I felt almost like a priest hearing confession. Then, after a time, the laughing and joshing ceased and all of us were silently watching the flames and embers for a long, long period. Suddenly Nick tore off all his clothes, and standing there naked, he raised his arms to the stars. "I'm clean!" he shouted. "I'm clean!" No one said anything and putting on his clothes he crawled under his blanket.

There are lots of different campfires: cooking fires, warming fires, sleeping fires, even survival fires. One of the latter occurred when a friend and I foolishly made a canoe trip down the upper Tioga in a November snowstorm to hunt ducks and geese. Trying to go around a big windfall snag, the current sucked us under and we overturned. I don't know how we managed to keep our shotguns or haul the canoe up on the bank or find the paddles that had floated downstream but we did. I do know that we were soaked to the hide and that our clothing was beginning to freeze hard when we attempted to make a fire.

Fortunately, I had a little bottle with six matches in it that were dry and by finding some cylinders of old white birch logs full of duff we soon had two little fires going, one for him to hover over and the other for me until our teeth had stopped chattering. Then we stripped in stages, wrung out our woolen underwear, socks and outer garments, put them on again, built a bigger fire and toasted ourselves alternately front and rear until we could bear to get in the canoe again. Paddling furiously to keep from congealing, we still had to make one other fire before we got back to the car.

Sleeping fires require a good back log, a big one that will hold the coals on its bottom edge and reflect the warmth all night. You collect a lot of dead maple saplings and line them up so you can push their ends into the fire when it dies down. One of the best ones I ever built was when I was going cross country to Lake Superior. At the edge of a small creek there was a stand of huge hemlock and white pines, the needles of which had carpeted the ground ten inches thick. Across the creek were a lot of small dead maples I could push over and haul to the fire site, but I couldn't find a big back log. Instead I found a big slab of slate colored rock and propped it up, then built a lean-to of branches and covered them with a heavy layer of the needles. It was very cold that night but I was snug as a bug in that shelter, so much so that I couldn't bear to leave the next morning. Often I dream of that spot and that fire with its comforting flicker of yellow and blue flames.

On another occasion when I was just exploring the forests I had an unusual experience. The little fire I'd built was in a small clearing near a swamp. I felt free but very much alone there in the wilderness. I wasn't. As I sat there watching the fir branches curl up into the *kuolema goru* (a Finnish phrase for the fists of death), suddenly a rabbit appeared at the edge of the firelit ground, then another, and still another. They kept darting in and out of the visible circle and there was once when I counted eight of them at one time. That never happened to me again and I cannot explain it. Were they just curious or were they telling me I was not alone? Is any one ever alone?

And I remember the campfire on the Slate River which flows into Lake Superior down a series of beautiful little cascades. Always one of my favorite places, I had brought my bride there so that she could learn to love the U.P. too. I'd made a little lean-to on a mossy rock outcropping near one of the river's little waterfalls with a campfire reflecting its warmth into it. The sound of the water and the clean air soon wrought their magic and she slept deeply while I watched the flames and embers. As a matter of fact I watched them all night long, constantly replenishing the wood as it burned down because a black bear kept grunting and snuffling at the edge of the firelight all night. My love never heard a thing and wondered why her new husband was so bleary-eyed when she awoke next morning.

Another campfire that I had to keep going all night was on the divide of land that separates the Lake Superior and Lake Michigan watersheds. Iggy Waisanen and I had been hiking for two days to the old slate mines near the ghost town of Arvon. At one time, shortly after the Civil War, they had produced some of the finest slate in the world and back then it was needed for blackboards, slate roofs, and the slates on which kids did their school lessons. The slate was loaded onto wagons pulled by mules down to Lake Superior where it was shipped on schooners to Detroit and Chicago via the Soo. Iggy and I did find the mines as well as some foundations of old buildings, collected some samples and then headed home through the forest.

That night we made a cooking and sleeping fire on top of a high hill after cleaning a wide space of leaves that had fallen from the towering maples all around us. Both of us were very tired and Iggy went to sleep immediately while I kept the fire going. Finally when it had burned down so that no sparks were to be seen I curled up in my own blanket. I do not know how long I slept or what awakened me but I awoke to find Iggy gone. Listening intently I heard something in the darkness far beyond the firelight and going to it I found my friend walking in his sleep saying "Where is he? Where is he?" Absolutely unresponsive to my shouting, he kept walking further into the hardwoods until I tackled him and sat on him until he woke. We had a difficult time finding the fire again. Indeed it looked like a tiny spark when I first spotted it. Iggy lay down and promptly went to sleep again but I sure didn't.

Oh yes, and there was that campfire we built every night outside my father's old hunting cabin when our three children were very young. As the darkness descended, the five of us sat there in the long grass watching the flames, occasionally feeding them with a sliver of cedar or a dead branch of reddish brown balsam, listening to the wild, lorn call of a loon on the lake as the night folded us into its arms. Oh what a feeling of unity came over us all as we saw the red embers form. The kids snuggled close when something rustled in the dark woods and then, when they couldn't stand it a minute more, they bolted into the cabin to hide under the safe blankets of their bunks, giggling deliciously until we joined them.

Another memory returns. (If I'm not careful I'll fall asleep). Every fall in November I return to Tioga and then head up in the bush to the cabin my father built over sixty years ago. Ostensibly I go to hunt deer but mainly for memories and good fellowship. With me are my son John, my son-in-law Tim, and Tim's Father Del. We have a ball together as only deer hunters will understand. Each year I try to bring up some odd kind of meat, whale, buffalo, rattle snake, alligator, whatever, in case we fail to get any venison. One year I lugged up a whole suckling pig. Because it was far too big to fit in our camp oven, I had "the boys" build one outside. Not much of an oven, either, it was mainly a trench lined with rocks, but they'd contrived a pole resting on two forked sticks that could turn the pig so it would be roasted on all sides.

To make sure that the oven would be hot enough, the boys built a monstrous fire in the trough and tended it in shifts all through the night to build up a substantial bank of coals. Next morning just as we skewered the pig on the turning pole it began to snow. Lord, how it snowed! By noon there were six inches on the ground; by six o'clock, fourteen. I was the only one hunting that day since it took the efforts of all the others to keep the fire going under the brush tent they'd erected. After the longest Happy Hour in the history of the north country, we brought the critter in about bedtime, stuck an apple in its snout, and tried to carve it.

The suckling pig was just like the World's Largest Pasty that Tioga's Pete Ramos once baked in a similar outdoor oven one Fourth of July. That pasty was raw on both ends and burnt in the middle, and so was our pig. We raised the flag on the camp flagpole and buried the beast under a pile of snow then ate pork and beans and went to bed. Didn't really matter. We sure had fun keeping that fire going in the snow.

In my first Northwoods Reader I told about Carl Anters, our town's mad young genius, who composed flame symphonies. Following his zany notion, I too have attempted to use fire as an art form and have enjoyed many pleasant hours not only outdoors but by our home fireplace carefully arranging the kindling, small wood and logs in unusual ways to get the effects I wanted. The compositions almost seem to blend music, painting and sculpture in an ever moving sequence of sound, color and form.

I've found that different kinds of wood produce different colors, pine for yellow flame, cherry for blue, oak for orange. There are grey flames too. Tamarack and osage orange produce the most sparks and the loudest ones for a crescendo effect; a stick of green wood of any kind creates the highest hissing frequencies. Placing your sticks in certain arrangements will create forked tongues of flame; in others, the flames are curled; in still others one can produce jets that spurt out laterally. The possibilities are endless. Thus far, I've only been able to create two compositions which I can repeat at will that have preludes, themes, variations on those themes, and a decent finale. Like Carl Anters I've been unable to come up with a coding or notation system akin to that used in music but I'm working on it. The poor man's art form: just build a fire. I invite you to join Carl and me in this crazy quest.

Psychologists tell us that some privileged persons have peak experiences in which they are transcended out of themselves. I have known only two and one of them involved a campfire. Let me tell you about it. I had been exploring the north country again, wandering the woods and swamps, trying to lose myself so I could find myself again, wondering what it would be like over the next granite hill. In a little glade surrounded by immense maple and yellow birch trees I made a balsam bed, assembling the tip branches so they slanted just right to produce a springy, fragrant mattress under my one blanket. It takes some time to make a good balsam bed so it was dark when I finished. I lit the sleeping fire and sat beside it for a long time watching the flames turn the wood into embers.

Suddenly something happened that is almost impossible to put into words though it's still as vivid as though it occurred yesterday. As I sat there, I gradually began to shrink in size and so did the fire while the big trees grew taller and taller. I could see that fire getting smaller and smaller and knew that I was getting smaller too. Then the fire and I were two tiny specks; and then we winked out just as sparks do when they rise and disappear.

I have no idea how long I'd been out of myself but suddenly there

I was again by the fire as though nothing had happened. But something had! I was filled with an exaltation I have never known before or since. I felt as though for a moment I had been merged with a mysterious force or spirit of unbelievable majesty, that I had become one with the universe. Oh, I hate what I'm writing because my words are so inadequate you will not understand.

Nor, for that matter, do I. Had I just dropped off to sleep? I do not believe it. When one awakes from sleep there is always a short period of drowsiness whereas when I regained my consciousness of self and surroundings I was more vividly alert than I have ever been, almost bursting with excitement.

Perhaps it was just auto-hypnosis? I had been focusing on the fire for a long time; perhaps the flames had hypnotized me? I can't believe that explanation either; it just doesn't account for that glorious feeling of ecstasy that suffused me.

Was it a religious experience? I'm not a religious person in the formal sense. I do not go to church though I often read from the Bible, the Koran, and other good books and have spent my life serving others in trouble. In my trance, if that is what it was, I heard no voice speaking to me such as the one St. Paul heard on the road to Damascus. All I know is that for a moment I had been transcended into something larger than myself. I cannot forget that peak experience there by that little campfire in the forest.

SKUNKED

More than anything else it was laughter that helped us make it through the winter in Tioga during the early years of this century. It was laughter that bound us together, helped us feel that we were not alone, reassured us that the encroaching forest would not overwhelm us all. When a lady on the St. Paul train asked Pete Ramos as he walked up the aisle of the railroad coach if one of the pasties he was selling was enough for one person and he roared, "Well it is if you aint a Goddam Hawg!" the tale of it brought grins up and down our hill street within an hour. When the new teacher from Down Below daintily nibbled "a black pine nut" from the little bag of deer turds she found on her desk in school, belly laughter could be heard all the way from the slaughter house in the valley to Eric Niemi's shack on Mud Lake. Not very funny, you say? I agree as of now, seventy years later, but way back then we had a greater need to laugh at almost anything halfway comical. It was our way of thumbing our noses as we tiptoed along the edge of survival.

We always enjoyed a well turned phrase with some wit in it. For example when Charley Olafson stumbled and fell on his face and Arvo said, "Don't use your nose for a cane, Charley!" we liked it well enough to say it thereafter whenever anyone fell. And when Mrs. Mattila remarked that her husband might be the head of the house but she was the neck that turned the head, that saying reverberated for years too. An outrageous fancy always tickled our funny bones so we prized Slimber Jim Vester's artistic lies and retold them over and over again with appreciation.

But the main vehicle of our humor, if that's what you could call it, was the practical joke. We called it "playing a trick" on one another. Everybody did it and that is why Halloween and April Fool's Day were our major holidays. Not that we confined our trickery to them either; we played practical jokes all year long. Some of the practical jokes were terribly crude, some ingeniously devised, but the code was that you had to take their consequences without getting mad. Just laugh with your tormentor, that's how you had to handle it, and plan to get even as soon as you could!

Our practical jokes ranged from the very simple to the complex. Examples of the simple ones would be the placing of a tack on the teacher's chair, or putting salt in the sugar bowl, or taking the tugs (traces) off the whiffletree of Old Man Marchand's mail wagon so that when he yelled "En avant! Giddyap" the horse would go, leaving the wagon behind and almost pulling the old man over the dashboard until he let go the reins. Pretty crude, but we were too.

Some of the more complex practical jokes took some real planning and executing - like the time we kids violated the Halloween curfew, and rang the school bell after midnight, almost driving Old Blue Balls crazy. Or, for example, when Pierre Valois spent the whole winter carving and painting a wooden head that looked just like his dead friend Henri Campeau, complete with handlebar mustachios. Pierre planted it in the graveyard right next to the tombstone. Sure shook you up to see Henri coming out of the ground. Pierre loved to watch people seeing it for the first time. I suppose it was more of a memorial than a joke, but Henri had played plenty tricks on Pierre in his time.

Of all the people in town Emil Olsen was the best - or worst- practical joker of them all. We were all wary of him, always. An ex-miner on a little pension, he seemed to devote his days to playing tricks or planning them. Why he even went to Ishpeming on the train and bought an exploding cigar and also an artificial flower to put in his lapel. It had a water bulb attached that he could hide inside his shirt. "Smell my flower!" he invited us, and when we did, we'd get a faceful of water. Oh, how the big Norwegian would laugh then. You could hear him all over town. Of course, the big folks soon heard about Emil's squirt flower so he couldn't suck them in so he had to try it on the little kids coming home from school until they caught on too.

The exploding cigar disappointed Emil. No one would accept it. Our men smoked Peerless or Granger in their corncob pipes. Hating to waste the money, Emil finally smoked it himself only to find that it was a dud - just fizzled out. Eino Tuomi, his friend and neighbor, almost laughed himself sick watching the flop, and couldn't help saying the same thing he'd said the previous April Fool's Day when Emil had tasted the stuff in the sap pail that Eino had hung from a spout on the telephone pole: "April Fool on you, Emil!" Usually Eino was the victim of Emil's tricks so he enjoyed it when Emil's victim was Emil.

One fine U.P. day in May Emil got an idea for a colossal practical joke that almost made him dizzy with its enormity. It came to him when he and Eino were sitting on Eino's porch watching the world go by. Part of that world was Pete Halfshoes, our resident Indian and, of course, when Emil saw him, he thought of Mabel. Everyone thought of Mabel when they saw Pete because Mabel was Pete's love and bed partner. Mabel was also a skunk, a lovely one with a white stripe all the way down its body and up its tail. The Chippewa Indian had found her when she was no larger than a tiny kitten and kept her, after removing the scent glands on each side of her anus, because the mice in his shack were driving him crazy. Not that Pete had any personal enmity toward mice or anything else but it's hell to sleep well when they run across your face. Besides you might be snoring with your mouth wide open.

Everybody liked Pete although some didn't approve of his life style. He'd been a soldier in the Spanish American War; he'd been a guide for the Huron Mountain Club; and he'd been a regular down at Higley's saloon ever since although he never had enough money at any one time to get really drunk. We kids liked to stop in at Pete's house to pet Mabel or to have Pete teach us animal tricks and woodlore. A nice, gentle old Indian, just as harmless as his skunk.

Well, the essence of Emil's practical joke, by far the best one he'd ever been able to think of, was that he'd live-trap a wild skunk and exchange it after dark for Mabel when Pete Halfshoes was still down at Higley's.

"No!" said Eino his friend and neighbor. "No! That no joke; that dirty trick. Pete, he good man, why you want stink up his house?" Always arguing anyway, Eino softly and Emil shouting, this time the wrangle continued for hours until finally the Norwegian stomped off in anger. "You Finns don't know what's funny," he said.

It's one thing to plan a practical joke and another to carry it out as Emil soon discovered. Though both he and Eino were good hunters and fishermen, neither had done trapping of any kind, least of all any live trapping. How do you make a live trap? Emil hated to ask anyone in town for fear that would give the joke away. He did know you had to have a good sized box and a trigger mechanism and the right kind of bait. The bait problem stymied him for a while until he met a man from Michigamme who told him what to do. "Use sardines for bait," the man said. "They're the best. Next best is a rotten chub or a handful of white grubs."

Emil had a tough time making the trigger because he forgot exactly how the man had described it. He had said you needed three hardwood sticks, one of them twenty inches long and each of the other two had to be a foot long. Then you had to carve shallow notches in them so that when assembled they made a figure four with the long stick horizontal. You put the bait on the inside end of the long stick, and propped the whole shebang upright at the middle of the tilted box's edge. When the animal you were trying to trap hit the bait, the whole figure-four stick trigger collapsed and the box came down with the critter inside. That's about all Emil remembered.

It took the old Norwegian about a week before he finally got the contraption working right. Eino wasn't any help at all; all he did was argue that it was a dirty trick to play on old Pete. He did suggest that although it would be easier to find a skunk down at the slaughter house, that would mean quite a carry, and besides he'd seen a skunk prowling around Emil's own chicken yard the night before.

So that's where Emil put the live-trap. A skunk had been around there all right as you could tell by the faint smell. Probably wanted to get in and rob a few eggs. The figure four trigger was hard to cock. You had to get the loose sticks so they fit together in the notches just right; the sardines kept falling off until he finally wired them on. Sure was a hair trigger though.

The next morning Emil was sure delighted. The box was down flush on the ground but when he gingerly lifted it up, the neighbor's cat ran out yowling. Good thing Emil hadn't eaten th rest of the sardines because the damned cat had made away with the bait. So he set it again and the following morning even before he got out of his bed Emil knew he'd caught a skunk. Phew! Eino came over mad as hell and told him to get the bugger out of there, that he could hardly breathe when he opened the door of his house, the stink was so strong. Then Eino returned to his house and slammed the door. It looked as though Emil's joke was going to end a long and beautiful friendship.

I guess Emil hadn't really thought things out. If he lifted the box the skunk would come out. The box had no floor, so he couldn't carry it up to Pete's place that night to let it loose in his house. What the hell to do? Emil went inside to think; the smell wasn't quite so strong there.

Finally, the solution came to him. He'd have to put the skunk in another box, one that had a floor and a lid that would stay down even if the skunk tried to lift it off. He'd put the animal in the new box and hide it in the grove until it was time to take it to Pete's house that night.

But how was he going to be able to make the transfer? Emil had heard tell that if you grabbed a skunk by the tail and held it high enough it couldn't spray, that it had to brace its hind legs on the ground to get the glands to squirt. Made sense, so Emil made a holding box with a lid and a latch. Eino didn't come out of his house next door to watch him, but Emil could see him looking out of the window now and then.

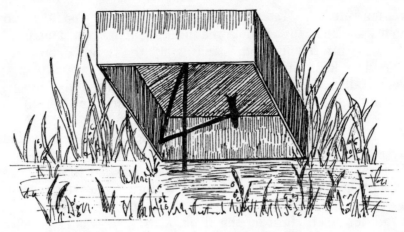

"Well, let's get it over with," said Emil to himself as he placed the holding box beside the live-trap. Out came the skunk with both cannons firing and Emil grabbed it by the tail, trying to hold it high, but the spray caught him and he couldn't see where the holding box was. When he put the skunk down he missed the opening and the skunk ran away. Skunks can move pretty fast when they have to.

Lord, what a stink! Emil was so thoroughly plastered, he took off all his clothes right there in the yard, ran to the rain barrel and using his shirt for a washcloth, scrubbed until he could see again. Then entering his house, he got a cake of laundry soap and washed himself from head to toe. He still stunk. Indeed he continued to stink every time it rained for a month afterwards. His clothing was such a disaster, he finally had to bury it after trying in vain to boil the aroma out on his kitchen range. All that did was to stink up the whole house. Eino wouldn't have a thing to do with him and every person he met on the street for a month thereafter held their noses. Higley kicked him out of the saloon when he tried to buy a beer. It was a tough time for Emil Olsen.

You might think that experience would have been the end of it but if so, you don't know Norwegians. When they start something, they finish it even if they destroy themselves and everyone else in the process.

Gradually, the skunk smell began to fade in the neighborhood and gradually Eino and Emil restored their old friendly relationship. It was like old times again, thought Eino one night when he and Emil staggered home from the saloon. The next morning, however, he saw the old Norwegian building something back of his house. It was a better live-trap for skunks. For one thing, Emil had built a box low enough in height so a skunk couldn't raise its tail. For another, it had a floor, and catches along the sides so that when the box came down it would lock tight. Emil had even contrived a handle so he could carry the thing. Eino tried his utmost to persuade Emil to do his trapping down by the slaughter house or anywhere else but the

Norwegian refused. "Too far to carry," he quoted. "Too far to carry."

So it was Eino's turn to do some thinking. How could he find some way to keep his friend from stinking up the neighborhood again? How could he keep that bullheaded Norwegian from polluting poor old Pete Halfshoes? Tough questions, those! The only thing Eino could think of was to stay up all night every night and let any skunk out of the live-trap that had got in. He tried that one night. Nothing came and Eino was pooped all the following day from loss of sleep. No there had to be a better way, if only he could think of it.

The day came at last when Emil was satisfied that he'd gotten all the bugs out of his new live trap. The figure four trigger worked like a dream; the slightest touch would collapse it and bring the box down to latch itself tight on the floor boards. It was low enough so the skunk couldn't possibly lift its tail high enough to spray. The handle was in place. Emil brought it over to Eino to admire but got no favorable response. That night he set it beside the chicken yard and cocked it with more sardines for bait.

The next morning the trap was sprung but there wasn't any smell. "Damn, I've caught that cat again," thought Emil but when he went to look through the porthole (another improvement he'd made) there was a good sized skunk inside. "Hurray for me!" he yelled. "Norway forever!" Eino came out of his house to look and, for once, didn't give out the same old lecture on not playing a dirty trick on Pete Halfshoes. Emil had no trouble at all when he carried the live-trap with the skunk in it up to the grove behind the Indian's shack. No skunk smell at all. Indeed the skunk didn't do anything but sleep as he carried it and hid the box.

Now the only things that could possibly go wrong were the possibility that Pete might not go to Higley's that night or that Mabel might not be around to be exchanged. Emil wasn't very worried about Pete not being at the saloon. Hell, he hadn't missed a Saturday night there in more than a year. As for Mabel, Pete never left her in the house when he was away; always put her out in the yard or left the gate open so she could run free. No, everything was set.

That night about ten o'clock when it was dusk but you could see, Emil retrieved the live-trap box from the grove where he'd hidden it and brought it up to Pete Halfshoes' shack. The door was closed, the gate was open, and there was no sign of Mabel in the yard. Probably out night-walking till Pete came home from the saloon. Emil carried the box to the door but stumbled on the step and swore. Suddenly, as he took the lid off, the door opened and there was Pete Halfshoes with a shotgun in his hand. Emil almost died with fright.

"Whatcha doin here?" Pete growled. Then the Indian saw the skunk coming out of the box. "Ah, Emil, my friend. You bring me back my Mabel, eh? Tanks!"

Consumed with horror but unable to move or say a word, Emil

watched as Pete picked up the wild skunk, petted it, and put it on his shoulder. Then Emil took off, running as fast as he could, waiting for the smell and the shotgun blast. He never stopped till he got home, and being out of booze went over to Eino's house to beg for a drink of whiskey and to tell him what had happened.

Eino heard him out and gave Emil a good shot of rot gut before he said, "Yah, Apil Fool again on you, Emil. That was no wild skunk. That was Mabel. I got her and put her in your trap when you went store."

THE TOM WOMAN

Generally speaking, our town was remarkably tolerant of those among us who were different, probably because of our ethnic mix. If old Viima claimed he heard voices telling him the world was coming to a bad end and that he'd better fix up his root cellar with bedding and food, well, that was all right. Little stunted Theodore Demar had been born that way. So what? He was a very smart kid in school. When a very bow-legged stranger got off the train at the depot, Pete Ramos quoted Shakespeare or somebody, "What manner of men are these that wear their balls in parentheses?" Pete wasn't being mean; he was just being curious.

Nevertheless, there were limits to our tolerance. If the deviance threatened our well being or our basic beliefs, then the full pressure of our town's disapproval made itself felt immediately. For one example, when Alphonse Carpentier, drunk as a hoot owl, careened down our hill street on his bicycle and severely injured a little boy playing on the sidewalk, the next day the wheels of that bicycle had disappeared and were never seen again.

One of our basic beliefs was that a boy is a boy, and a girl a girl, a man a man, and a woman, being double-breasted, belonged in the kitchen and the bed. Tioga had no woman's lib. The only instance of it I can recall is when Mrs. Manginen, tired of following her man to church, ran ahead of him and tried to sit in the men's section. Of course, he threw her out bodily. No, women were expected to act like women. It was the unwritten law.

Tekla Toivisto came into the world kicking, screaming, and fighting. My father, who had delivered thousands of babies, said he'd never seen one so furious. What is more, the little girl baby raised cain throughout her infancy. Her mother who had looked forward with great eagerness to having a girl after two sons could hardly hold her, she struggled so. She yelled and cried almost the entire time she was awake. They wrapped her in swaddling cloths to restrain her. My father was called to see if she had colic or something but she didn't. She'd outgrow it, he said. Oddly, the only time she was quiet was in her father's arms; he alone could calm her. Tekla's first teeth came in at four months and she promptly bit her mother's nipples so hard they had to put her on cow's milk.

Once Tekla learned to walk, and she walked early, it was hard to control her, the mother said. She was always climbing something or smashing something else. She wouldn't play with dolls except to use them as hammers. Her frequent temper tantrums and obstinacy made her mother's life miserable but the girl never showed such behavior in front of her father. Indeed, she would do anything to be able to sit on his lap or wrestle with him on the floor. She refused to let her mother hug or kiss her but she showed extreme affection to her father, and sometimes to her older brothers. When another girl baby was born to the Toivistos they expected trouble but Tekla simply ignored her completely. Altogether she was a strange child, Tekla was.

When it came time for Tekla to go to school her mother had a real battle getting her to put on the new dress and wear the bow of red ribbon in her hair. Combing and brushing her hair had always been an ordeal but this time her mother had to straddle her on the floor to get the job done. One of her brothers, assigned to take her to school that first day, returned shortly saying that Tekla had rolled in the mud and run away before he got her there. Mrs. Toivisto found Tekla, gave her a hard spanking, washed and ironed the dress and took her back right into the schoolroom. At recess Tekla came home again, all dirty again, and her mother wept. However, that night her father talked to Tekla about school and how he wanted her to be good and please not to shame him again. After he personally took Tekla to school the next day, there was no further difficulty.

The early years of grade school were happy ones for the girl, probably the only ones she was ever to have, because the boys accepted her as one of them. They called her Tom for tomboy because she could do anything they could do and often do it better. Tucking her yellow pigtail braids inside one of her brother's old caps and wearing his outgrown overalls, she almost looked like a boy. She could run faster, jump further, and fight harder too. She beat up the bully who pestered their gang so thoroughly he never bothered them again. Tekla never threw side-arm like most girls do; she threw overhand so swiftly the team that won the one-hand-over-the-other-up-the-bat always picked Tekla as their pitcher. She wasn't afraid to talk tough and swear. On skis she was a daredevil going down the steepest hills and trying the biggest jumps. If she fell, she never cried.

Things changed when adolescence came. The boys no longer wanted to play childish games with her; they were becoming men. Although Tekla could shoot straighter with a slingshot than any of them, they excluded her from their hunts. When they build a ramshackle shack down in the grove, they put up a crudely lettered sign that read: "No girls aloud! This means YOU" An invisible barrier had been erected that Tekla couldn't pierce. She began to hate herself for being a girl, almost as strongly as she hated most of the other girls. When little bumps began to swell on her chest, she was furious. "I won't have boobies! I won't have them!" she screamed to her mother once and nothing her mother could say could calm her. For months Tekla wore a canvas band cut from an old tent. This she bound so tightly across her breasts deep lines were left when she took it off. When finally it became apparent that nothing worked, Tekla went around wearing a very loose sweater to hide the swellings.

Very lonely, Tekla turned to her father for companionship and, knowing the girl was having a rough time, he spent all the time he could spare with her. The two of them hunted and fished together. When Tekla shot her first buck at fifteen she insisted on cleaning, skinning and butchering it herself, though she let her father provide the instructions. With him she learned to spear suckers or net them. He showed her how to find good water at the edge of a lake or swamp, how to run a line surveying timber. She helped him cut trees with a two-man crosscut saw and when she found herself awearying, she spent a lot of free time lifting stones to strengthen herself.

The high point of Tekla's High School years was the week her father took her out of school to spend on the trapline with him. It was sheer bliss. He taught her all the lore he knew: how to read animal tracks, how to make the different kinds of sets in the proper places, how to skin a pelt, even how to cook, an accomplishment she had previously spurned. When the week ended Tekla could hardly bear to come out of the woods.

In High School too, Tekla had her first and only date - if that is what you might possibly call it. One of the boys she had played with in grade school asked her to go trout fishing with him. Pierre Tremblant was a tall handsome French Canadian kid. He was also a wild one, always out to get a little nooky if he could, and he'd noticed Tekla's golden hair and fine figure. Well, they had a fine gay afternoon and evening on Wolf Creek even though Tekla fished rings around him but when he tried to feel her up and kiss her she slugged Pierre so hard he almost swallowed his eyeballs. That ended that!

Having more one hundreds than anyone in her graduating class, Tekla was chosen valedictorian. That meant she had to read an original composition before everyone assembled in the Town Hall. It was the custom, the evidence that one had truly been educated. Although miserable in a new dress and resenting her high heels, she really looked pretty up there on the platform. I forget the title of her composition but its theme was that a difference to be a difference must make a difference. Our people didn't understand a word of it, but they all applauded. It meant that the program was almost over and that soon they could take off their tight shoes too.

Most of our girls, after they graduated from high school, soon got married or they left to find household jobs in the big cities down below. Or they became teachers. Tekla didn't want to go to any city; she loved the woods and waters too much. Being a hired girl sure didn't appeal to her either. As for marriage, that was out! She didn't want to teach but that seemed to be the only way to make a living. It was hell to be female! She was scorned and laughed at when she tried to get a job in the woods although she could do anything any man could do and do it better. What man would lower himself by having a woman on the other end of the crosscut saw? A woman in a lumber-camp? It was unthinkable. Maybe in the cook shack - but that was not for Tekla. After spending the summer after graduation making winter wood and picking berries for sale, she had made only thirty dollars so her father borrowed some money and sent her to the Normal School at Marquette to become a teacher.

That took two miserable years. Working part time by cleaning the gymnasium and locker rooms and toilets, and occasionally escaping to walk in the island park of Presque Isle, she endured and finally got her life certificate, but there were times on the long breakwater into Lake Superior when she'd been tempted to jump off and end it all. The only reason she didn't was that she knew she'd start swimming immediately, and besides she had to pay her father back. So she took a job teaching in a one room country school in Pelkie, a Finnish farming community.

That too was a most unpleasant year. "Miss Toivisto, Miss Toivisto," how she hated to hear those words! She didn't mind having to build her own fires or carry the water or even the teaching itself, but being cooped up in the little school building with twenty seven children all day long really irked her. Then too she had to board and room with a family that had hardly enough space for the parents and her, to say nothing about room for seven children, five of whom slept in the barn loft. All year long Tekla kept saying Sisu! Sisu! to herself and saving every penny of her meager salary. At the end of the year, the schoolboard did not invite her back and Tekla was relieved. She wasn't meant to be a teacher any more than she was meant to be a woman.

When she paid off the loan money and told her father she would never teach again, he looked sad but said that she could stay home as long as she wanted to. "The two boys are gone," he sighed, "and there's lots to do. You make the wood for winter and make the hay and raise the garden and bring home fish and meat. Maybe next fall you and me can go trapping again." He showed that he wasn't upset, just sorry for her. She saw the tears in his eyes when she told him she'd try to pay room and board.

And she did. It came about this way. One afternoon when she was cutting across Alex Olmstead's farm to pick berries on the granite bluffs, she heard moaning and cries for help. Responding, she found old Alex pinned down by a big timber that was part of an outbuilding he'd been razing. Somehow, by using a long log as a pry bar, she was able to free him. Afraid to move the old man who lay there moaning, she ran to town to get my father and returned with him. Alex had a broken leg and terrible bruises but he'd be all right in a month or so, Dad said, but only if he stayed in bed and had someone to take care of him. Knowing Tekla's situation, he suggested to Alex that he hire her. The old man readily agreed. "I pay you sixty dollars a month," he said. Having been getting only fifty cents for a ten quart pail of blueberries, Tekla jumped at the opportunity. Now she could pay board and room money.

Until his kids left and his wife died some fifteen years earlier Alex Olmstead had one of the finest farms in the area. Good loam-clay soil with all the rocks out of it had supported a fine dairy operation but Alex had grown old and discouraged. Some of the farther fields, once lush with alfalfa, were weed grown with little firs and brush coming in from the edges. He'd sold all the cows but one milker for his own use because the haying and care of them were more than his fading strength could handle. Alex still had an old horse that he used mainly to come to town with or to haul manure but the fences were sagging, and the barns needed painting and repairing. Too much to do, said Alex, and not enough strength at seventy-seven to do it. He was very much alone. Hadn't heard from his kids in ten years.

Tekla proved to be just what he needed. She cleaned the house and barn till they shone; she cooked his meals, nothing fancy but good substantial ones; she milked the cow and fed the horse. Once he asked her if she could fix the gate to the barnyard. Tekla not only did that but also put in fenceposts and tightened the barbed wire around both it and the first field. Alex was delighted.

When the month of convalescence was over and he was able to do a little work again, Alex asked Tekla to stay on, saying he'd pay her eighty dollars a month for her services. Again she accepted. Tekla was happier than she'd been for years. There was so much that needed doing and besides she was getting fond of the old man, almost as though she'd gotten a second father, almost one as good as her own. As for Alex, he was happier than he'd been for a long time too. Now he had someone to talk to again, someone who cared about him and his farm. The thought of having her leave was unbearable, but realistically he knew he wouldn't be able to keep that beautiful young woman very long.

So he asked her to marry him and said he'd put the farm in her name. Said he didn't need sex, that he was impotent. And said he just loved having her near him. Tekla asked for time to think it over, but, in the end, again she accepted. They went to Ishpeming to have a justice of the peace join them and a lawyer to change the will. Oh how the people in Tioga yakked but most of them approved. Made sense, an arrangement like that. Tekla was surprised to find that now the town accepted her. The rejection she had known all her life seemed to fade and disappear. It was odd how just adding the three little letters of Mrs. had caused her difference not to be difference.

Alex took some kidding, of course, when he went to town.

"That pretty young woman, she stiffen yer pecker, Alex?" one man asked.

"No," said Alex. "She's no woman. She's my son. Best son I ever had."

Two years later Alex died and Tekla took over. Hiring help when she needed it, in a few years she had built up that farm so it raised the best potatoes in the whole U.P. When someone asked one of her hired men how it was to work for a woman, he said, "She's fair enough, but a hard man to work for."

THE THUNDERBOLT

After his wife died and he began to have heart troubles my beloved Grandpa Gage came to live with us. Remembering the glorious times he and I had known together during previous visits I was overjoyed at the prospect but when he arrived, things had changed or he had changed. No longer was he that wild, zany Grandpa with whom I have done the Dance of the Wild Cucumber atop of Mt. Baldy. Indeed it was even hard for him to walk with me in the grove because he kept getting out of breath. When he sat down I could tell he was hurting. He didn't even look the same. His mustache now was completely white rather than gray, and his cheeks, once rosy, looked as though they were made of shiny grey wax. He was thinner too. When he filled his old pipe his hands shook so hard he had to use several matches to light it.

Oh there were times, a few of them when we were alone, when we recaptured some of our former gay spirits. Once he asked me if I had a girl friend yet and when I said no, that the girls didn't seem interested in me and that I was pretty shy around them, "Mr. McGillicuddy," he roared (or tried to). "Confidence! Mr. McGillicuddy, Confidence! I will now teach you a little song which you shall sing to yourself silently whenever a pretty girl goes by." He summoned up some energy and sang this in a quavering old voice:

"They'll go wild, simply wild over me.
Why they do is sure a mystery.
They'll look at me and sigh,

In my arms they'll want to die,
They'll go wild, simply wild over me."

Exhausted, he took a little white pill out of a tiny bottle and put it under his tongue.

My mother tried to help me understand. "Cully," she said, "Your grandfather's very sick and he's very old. He just can't play with you as he did before. I know he'd like to, but he can't. You mustn't bother him any more than you can help, especially when he's napping." Grandpa seemed always to be napping either on the couch or up in his bedroom. I'd go upstairs and peek around the door, then sit there on the floor until he woke. Mother caught me doing that once and talked to me again.

"Cully," she said, and I could see tears in her eyes, "I've got to tell you that your Grandfather is probably not going to be with us much longer. He's going to die." Seeing the stricken look on my face, she fled.

I was furious. No! My grandpa wasn't going to die! I wouldn't let him! He was my Grandpa. He'd get well and then we'd have fun together again. Weeping up there in the back bedroom, I resolved to pray him back to health. God wouldn't let Grandpa die if I prayed hard enough.

So I prayed and I prayed, first thing in the morning and last time at night, and an awful lot of times in between. I went to the grove and to Mt. Baldy and all the other places where Grandpa and I had been together and at each one I begged God to make my Grandpa well. Each morning I hoped to find Grandpa looking better; every time he napped, I feared he might not wake up, that he'd be dead. Dead? That couldn't happen if I prayed enough.

But it did! One night, Mother awakened me from my sleep, held me in her arms like she did when I was little, and told me that Grandpa had died. She held me tightly there on my bed until my eyes could make no more tears. When she left, I lay on my wet pillow thinking I had not prayed hard enough. Finally I slept.

I won't go into what happened after that except that they made me go in to see my grandfather before they took him away. He seemed to be sleeping but his chest wasn't moving. All I can remember is that there seemed to be that same little crooked smile on his face that he'd always had when we were up to some devilment.

Time heals, so they say, but it was months before the emptiness left me. And the unfairness! It wasn't right that my Grandpa Gage should be dead. Why hadn't God listened to me?

One rainy day when I was reading one of the books Grandpa had given me a terrible thought came into my mind. The book was a collection of Greek myths, most of which weren't particularly interesting until I came to page 87 where it told about how Ajax challenged Zeus, the God of Gods, by going up on a mountain top, baring his breast, and daring Zeus to strike him down with a thunderbolt. For some reason that story stayed with me a long time. I just couldn't forget it.

And so one afternoon I walked down to the Methodist church, entered the door which was always open and committed the ultimate sacrilege. Petrified with fright, I went down the aisle between the empty pews and stood there facing the altar and the big arch behind it. My hands were shaking so I could hardly unbutton my jacket and shirt but finally I did and then baring my chest, I said, "Dear God. I prayed and prayed that you wouldn't let my Grandpa die but you did."

I remember that awful silence. No thunderbolt, just a scared little boy in an empty church. Then I looked up at the crest of the arch and cried, "I don't think you're there. I don't think you're you! I don't think there is a God!" Sobbing, I turned and ran down the aisle and out of the church, my jacket flapping and I hid in the hay mow until supper time waiting for the thunderbolt.

The sky was clear and although I was still scared, I also felt a little like Ajax until suddenly the terrible thought came to me that of course God wasn't there in the church on weekdays. That was why I'd been able to get away with it but come Sunday He would be in His House and then He'd get me!

On Sunday I pretended to be sick so convincingly that my father gave me calomel and castor oil to clean me out and told me to stay in bed all day, which I did very willingly. That night I prayed asking for forgiveness but I thought that if He hadn't let my grandpa live He would be unlikely to answer that prayer either. The next Sunday I played sick again, the Sunday after that again, but the following Sunday my mother just made me go with her although she must have known how frightened I was - even if she hadn't known why.

It didn't look good either. It was a very dark day with heavy black low clouds and the rumble of thunder in the west. My terror made me sit very close to my mother. Even if I'd been bad, *she* was good and He wouldn't want to hurt *her*. I clutched her skirt, pressing my face against her side. The sermon seemed to be lasting forever when the rain began. I could hear it on the roof. Soon there were some flashes of lightning followed by loud thunder. Mother put her arms around me in the pew. Then there came a terrible flash of lightning with a thunderbolt almost simultaneously. The biggest bang in the world!

The preacher and half the congregation were on their knees but I was under the pew with my hands over my head, waiting, waiting. Mother, recognized my utter terror, picked me up and left the church. As we went out the door, we saw that the lightning had struck a large maple tree in the church yard, splitting its trunk into long strips. To herself mother said aloud, "There'll be less sinning among the congregation next week." I barely heard her. All I could think of were two words: "He missed!" Somehow I had the feeling that he wouldn't waste another thunderbolt on a little boy no matter how bad he'd been.

But Grandpa Gage was dead.

RECIPE FOR A HAPPY MARRIAGE

Next year I shall be eighty years old, most of which were spent in the pursuit of folly and the cultivation of a gay spirit. Certainly my white beard makes me look wiser than I am but one bit of wisdom I feel I have acquired. It is this. The only successful and happy marriages are those in which both the husband and wife share the *illusion* that he is the boss. The important point is that it must be an illusion shared by both.

This is the tale of John Pelkie and his wife Lena. When they married at nineteen our people in Tioga grinned a bit because he was only five feet four in height while she was a strapping six feet one. A short man has to climb a mountain, they said. It was just nature's way of evening things up. They'd have no trouble fitting inside the same bed and their children would be sized in between. No problem. It would be a good marriage, people said.

Had our people thought a bit more deeply about it, they could have seen trouble signs. Lena came from a home where the man was boss, the big boss. There was no illusion about it. Her father's word was law; his wish was everyone's command. Not only his wife but his children feared his sudden temper and the heavy blows that went with it. In the Tioga of today the couple would have been divorced before their first wedding anniversary but back then divorce was viewed as utterly shameful in the U.P. To be known as a divorcee was almost as bad as being known as a prostitute. Once you were married it was "until death do you part."

Of course there were marriages so terribly intolerable they just could not be endured. When that happened, the man just took off for parts unknown and never came back again. After a decent interval of ten years or so, he was presumed dead, and the woman, if she had the heart for it, would marry another man and no one thought anything of it. What if the man didn't go? Well, Mrs. Durosa willingly went to prison for ten years after shooting her man in the head, the heart and the stomach sequentially. When she finally got out, she said jail hadn't been too bad in comparison.

In most cases, however, bad marriages were simply endured. It was "Sisu!" You'd made your bed and had to lie in it. That's the way it had been in Lena's home. Never once had her mother complained even to her about her father's abuse. Lena had watched her grow old before her time, worn to the bone trying to please the man, and never managing to do it. Often she had despised her mother's weak submission. No, when Lena got married, things would be different. No man was going to dominate her!

The situation in John Pelkie's home had been almost the opposite. Everyone in Tioga knew that his father was the most hen-pecked man in town. There were a few others but their wives had sense enough not to parade their dominance in public. Not John's mother! In the store, on the church steps, almost anywhere there were people to watch, she humiliated him. She treated him like a dog, people said, making him heel upon command. Moreover, she constantly abused him in public verbally, parading his weaknesses, constantly belittling him. "If she were my wife, I'd punch her in the nose," a lot of our men said contemptuously. In the early years of this century the U.P. was a man's world. Being macho was just being natural.

All the time John Pelkie was growing up he was ashamed of his father. Rarely would he invite his friends to come to his house. It hadn't been so bad when he was little to hear his mother giving his father fits. After all, she gave all the kids hell too. But when John got to be twelve or so, he sure resented it. Often he could barely restrain himself from saying, "Shut up, aitee (mother); leave him alone!" but he knew that would shame his father even more. Why didn't he hit her? Why did he always just sit and take it?

Well, with that background, you can understand why John Pelkie was going to make very sure that his new wife wasn't going to push him around even if she were bigger than he was. No sir! HE was going to be the boss. He'd told her so, too. Lena didn't argue the point but she did lift a lovely eyebrow. After all they weren't married yet when he laid down that law.

Most of us in Tioga didn't have a honeymoon after we got married. We just moved into the house and started living and fighting together. John and Lena, however, did have a semblance of one. They loaded their packsacks and hiked up to a little vacant trapper's cabin at the headwaters of the Tioga River. There they spent a week looking over the country to see if it might be worthwhile to set up a trapline there the following fall. The Pelkies had their first argument even before they started walking when John insisted on carrying a heavier load than Lena. He won that little battle, he thought, until he saw her pick up a large rock and put it in her packsack.

It was a long hike, more than nine miles. At first they followed an old logging road and as they walked side by side John found it hard to keep up, she took such long strides. Therefore when the trail narrowed he made damned sure he went first. After the first hour when the straps were cutting into his shoulders he said, "You getting tired, I think. We take a rest." It sure irritated him when Lena protested that she wasn't tired at all. By the time they finally reached the trapper's shack, John was pretty well bushed but not so tired that he didn't brush her off when she tried to help him take off his heavy packsack. He also hated himself when he staggered and almost fell forward when the burden was off his back while she swung hers off without any trouble.

"How you like that, Lena?" he asked, pointing to the lake lined with birch and fir trees with a little stream flowing out of it past the cabin. "I like it very much, Johnny," she replied. He didn't like that Johnny business. His name was John Pelkie and later on he'd tell her so.

The shack wasn't much from the outside though it seemed to have a good roof but when they went through the half opened door they found a real mess. The porkies had gotten in and made a shambles of the place. Their crap was everywhere, on the floor, the table and the bunk. They had chewed the rungs of the two chairs as well as the centerpost. Even the coffeepot and skillet showed the scraping of their teeth marks. "OK," said Lena. "We clean up!" John was glad the mess hadn't upset his new bride but he didn't like that "We." Cleaning was woman's work. There was no broom. "I make you broom, Lena," he said.

However, by the time he'd gathered and cut the willows, and bound them together around a pole after splitting them lengthwise, Lena had used an old sack to get the cabin remarkably clean. She even had hauled the old mattress from the bunk and was beating it with a pole as it leaned against a tree. Together they took the blankets and things out of the packsacks. "Now you get out, Johnny. Take a walk. I fix things up." Good," he thought, "she knows her job." But he didn't particularly like the way she was already bossing him around.

It was dark when returning, he saw the candle light in the window. The cabin sure looked nice with strings of groundpine on the table set with clean cups of stream water and plates that were filled with cold pork and beans, korpua and a chunk of jelly. Lena apologized for the meal. "I cook you a good breakfast tomorrow, Johhny," she said. "Stovepipes no good. We have to cook outside."

Their marriage night was not too good because John was still too pooped. Finally he climbed the mountain and all was well.

Breakfast was a disaster. Lena, always an early to bed, early to rise person, had arisen shortly after dawn to build a fire outside and cook the bacon, pancakes and coffee. John, a late to bed and to rise man, kept snoring hour after hour, so she ate alone, did her dishes in the creek and walked along the shore of the lake watching the loons before finally awakening him. He was grumpy when he awoke but plain nasty when he saw his breakfast. God, the bacon was so crisp it almost broke his teeth; the pancakes were too thick. He liked thin ones; the coffee was too weak. When he told her so, she dumped the batter and the coffee and the bacon into the fire and told him he could damn well make his own breakfast. Then she went into the shack and wept a little.

That afternoon the two of them spent exploring the south shore of the lake looking for animal signs and places where John might set his traps the next fall. To John, it felt good to be teaching her so many new things and answering her questions. Somehow when he was in that role he felt taller. "How would you like some wild potatoes to go with the fried bologna for supper?" he asked.

"There aren't any potatoes up here in the bush," she protested.

"No, but there's something almost as good - spatterdock roots. I saw some of their pads this morning in the bay by the outlet. Let's go get some." John led the way to where the yellow-cupped lily pads covered the surface of the lake. "Might as well take off all our clothes," he said. "We may have to grub around in the mud for the roots. They're long and knobby."

So there they were, naked as Adam and Eve in Paradise, gathering their evening food. After they had enough roots for several meals deposited on shore they swam far out in the lake to cleanse themselves. Lena was the better swimmer but, managing to get back about the same time she did, he put his arms around her to feel her breasts.

"Those aren't wild potatoes!" she yelled, whirling around. Then she picked him up and threw him bodily ten feet away from her into the water. "Wow! she's strong," John thought. Lena also was beautiful. He could hardly keep his hands off the tall woman with the yellow wet hair streaming over her shoulders, but she pushed him away. "I'm no mink to be mated on the beach," she said. "In bed OK." And that night it was until she tried to get on top. John flung her off him and, putting on his clothes, spent almost an hour outside the cabin in the dark. She was asleep when he came inside but he found it hard to stop thinking until long after midnight.

Breakfast that next morning wasn't as bad as it had been the last time. Lena managed to cook the bacon to suit him but not the oatmeal. She liked hers soupy; she found he wanted his granular, and neither was particularly tasty because all they had to put on it were sugar and condensed milk diluted with water. Lena had made the coffee stronger than suited her but he let her know he wanted it stronger yet. He also told her she didn't know how to build a cooking fire, that the best way was to put two logs in parallel with the fire in between, that you had to cook with coals, not flames, and that the best wood for coals was dry maple, not the spruce and cedar junk stuff she was using. Somehow she managed to keep her mouth shut but inside she was furious.

Well that's the way the honeymoon week went. Some good moments and some, perhaps more, lousy ones. Lena returned feeling that she had married the wrong man. Often during the week she had thought "He sounds just like my father" or "He treats me as though I were dumb or something" and "Who is he to be so bossy?" She resented strongly his apparent need to dominate her. She was damned if she'd be like her own mother and always give in. At least he hadn't tried to abuse her physically. Good thing he hadn't tried. She would have knocked his block off. She knew she could. There was a bit of comfort in that.

John came back from the honeymoon feeling fairly good. On the one hand, he hadn't let Lena boss him around; if anything, he'd done the bossing. On the other hand there was a vague feeling that his dominance might not last very long. She was a strong woman and although she'd gone along with his demands and criticisms, still that might have been due to the fact that they'd been up there in the bush where everything was as new to her as it was familiar to him. He had managed to be king up there but would he rule the kingdom in town? "Well," he thought, "I damn right will!"

One of the first things Lena did was to go to see Mrs. Mattila, she who had authored the town-saying of "He thinks he's the head of the house, but I'm the neck that turns the head." Lena told the wise old woman about the honeymoon and the relationships between her weak mother and cruel domineering father. She told her about the fears she had that John might turn out to be like her father. She didn't want to live a life like her mother had known. Lena asked Mrs. Mattila for advice.

Mrs. Mattila listened until Lena's well ran dry. "I have lived a long time," she said. "I have seen some good husbands and some bad ones. Good husbands aren't born; they are made - by their wives. They're all babies underneath and have to be trained. You can make your John into just the kind of man you want him to be - if you know what you want." The old lady lit her corncob pipe and blew a few smoke rings.

"Now listen well for I will not say it again. The first thing is to give him permission to do the things he's planning to do anyway. Or suggest to him that he do them. You will do that exactly twenty three times a day for the first month and eleven times a day for second month. By the end of that time he will, for the most part, be doing whatever you want him to do."

At that point Mr. Mattila came into the kitchen. "Arvo," said the old lady, "The horse needs to be currycombed and the harness oiled before we take the buggy to church tomorrow, don't you think, yes?" "Yah," said Arvo. "I do it." Mrs. Mattila gave Lena a wink.

"Now for the second thing," she continued. "Give him lots of love and babying, but use them! They shouldn't be free stuff. Hold back if he doesn't deserve it but give plenty if he does. And that's not just in bed but outside it too. Find out how to show affection - touch on cheek or head, tell him he's big stuff, give hug and such. If he pouts, you just wait. If he angry, you put his words in your mouth and show you know how he feel. Feed him good."

Mrs. Mattila relit her pipe and grinned. "Now for the third thing, the last one," she said. "A man has some wolf in him always. That part can never be tamed. There will come times when he needs to run free with the pack or alone. Let him have rope. Just tug it a little, then let him go. And when he comes back to you, as he will, do not give him the length of your hot tongue or shame him for he already has shame enough." The old lady went over to the range, lifted a lid and knocked the goo out of her corncob. The interview was over.

Lena eagerly put the three principles into practice, and John never knew what happened to him. He had feared getting married but he'd never been so happy in his life. Oh, they fought occasionally, usually about something that seemed trivial the next morning. Yes, there were times when Lena almost sounded like his mother did when she gave his father hail Columbia, but all in all there was peace in the valley. He noticed that the oatmeal was gradually getting a bit soupier and the bacon a bit crispier but that was OK. Everything was OK, even the applesauce which he preferred thick and she thin. When he climbed the mountain, the mountain didn't climb over him. Sure, he was the boss but that didn't really matter any more. Married life was good!

It was pretty good for Lena too but she didn't feel quite right about the way she'd been training John. It just seemed sort of sneaky even though it worked. He was so good to her now she felt guilty. No, things weren't right. Not enough excitement, too much contentment. Anything she wanted him to do, he did. Why didn't he give her hell once in a while? Why did he always give in?

One night when they were abed, all these feelings boiled over. Sounding almost like his mother, Lena gave John blue hell, bringing up all his faults and deficiencies, telling him he was as weak as his father, telling him he wasn't the man she thought she had married. On and on she went, getting angrier by the minute. Finally when she slapped his face right there in bed she said, "Hit me! Hit me, if you dare!"

John threw off the covers, turned her over and spanked her lovely buttocks so hard they turned red as a U.P. sunset. "Hit me again, John," she begged. It was "John", not "Johnny"? Joyously, he spanked that bottom until he saw the smile creep over her face. The loving that came afterwards was the best either had known. All was well.

She had regained the illusion, and he had maintained the illusion that the man was the boss.

THE MEDICINE MEN

 y father, Dr. Gage, was the only physician in Tioga. He served a territory as large as the state of Rhode Island if you count the uninhabited forests that surrounded our village. When he came to Tioga in the year 1900 all the mines were still working and the white pine was still being cut north of town. However, when the mines shut down and many of our inhabitants left, Dad stayed on, tending his people with a dedication we rarely see nowadays. Never did he send a bill for his services. "Pay me when you can" was his reply when someone said he didn't have the money to pay his modest fees of two dollars for an office call, five for a home visit, and ten dollars for a baby case. He delivered babies in the upper bunks of isolated cabins, performed appendectomies and other major surgery on kitchen tables if need be, and kept two horses tired to the bone making home calls. Often

we kids never saw our father for days when epidemics of flu or diphtheria raged like a forest fire through Tioga and neighboring towns. His people respected, even revered him, knowing that he would come, day or night, to tend them in their need.

Dad had little time for himself but when he had some, he spent it joyfully in hunting and fishing. The only other hobby he had, except reading, was doing magic tricks. He said that he'd started doing them in medical school to develop the eye-hand coordination a doctor needs when sewing up a wound or setting a broken bone. Dad could hold up a silver dollar in one hand, make a pass across it with the other hand, and Lo! it had disappeared.

There were a lot of other tricks too but the one I remember best was his belt trick. He'd take off his belt, double it, fold back the far end to make three little loops, then ask me to put a pencil through the loop I thought was the original one as he revolved the belt coil in his hands. Never could I get it in the right loop even though I held the pencil on both ends and was sure that I'd picked it. When Dad uncoiled the belt it just snaked off that pencil clean as could be. Then my father would laugh. "The hand, my friend, is quicker than the eye!" he would say. It sure was. I never figured out how he did it until I was in college and he showed me.

Dad was also interested in folk medicine. There was a lot of it in Tioga. The hairy plantain, a weed, would stop bleeding better than any pressure bandage, according to the Finns, and it really did. Dad used to grind some of it with his mortar and pestle to mix with an antiseptic ointment. The French Canadians and Indians had many concoctions of herbs and roots that they drank when having stomach distress, I mean belly aches. Dad frowned on their practice of putting axle grease or a cud of chewing tobacco on a gaping wound but he approved when an old Frenchman buried himself naked in a manure pile. "That moist heat probably does help his rheumatism," Dad said.

Long before the term "psychosomatic" had been coined, my father knew how important a part psychological and emotional factors could play. "Medicine is five percent broken bones, five percent surgery, ten percent delivering babies, and eighty percent humbug," he once confided to me. He didn't really believe that but it showed his appreciation of the role that faith contributes to the healing process. Always he would listen carefully to the patient's descriptions of his symptoms and probe for more. Then he would ask "How are your bowels?", say, "Let me see your tongue," then feel the pulse and listen to the heart with his stethoscope. "That stethoscope is the best drug in my satchel," he remarked.

That satchel was something too. When it was opened the trays of little bottles, filled with pills of different sizes and colors, were very impressive. My father at first had to make his own pills, mixing the ingredients including coloring extracts in the mortar, then rolling bits of the stuff between his thumb and forefinger into little balls which he squashed down on a marble slab. Then they were baked in our home's oven on a cookie sheet. Dad had seven colors of aspirin and three colors of sugar pills. The purple ones worked best, Dad said. One man, who'd left town when the mines closed and moved to California, used to send Dad an order every year for the purple ones. My father also mixed his liquid medications, measuring them carefully in a glass beaker, and after shaking thoroughly, poured them into various sized bottles. Usually he tasted them first to make sure they tasted bad enough, yet had sufficient alcohol to sting.

The old mining hospital where Dad mixed his medicines and held office hours was just across the street from my home. It was a wonderous forbidden place for a kid to explore and play when my father was away making house calls. One wing held the living quarters where the male nurse and caretaker had resided. Another wing had two large wards full of beds, and in the center section was the operating room with white tables and cupboards full of bone saws, forceps, knives and bandages.

Across the hall in this center section was the dispensary with the walls lined with shelves full of tall bottles holding drugs. All these bottles bore Latin descriptions of the drugs within them except for two that were labeled "Scotch Whiskey" and "Bourbon Whiskey." Dad told me they did have whiskey in them but one also had ipecac and the other croton oil. Ipecac makes you vomit and croton oil is probably the fastest, most powerful laxative known to sinners. Dad said he'd never had any trouble with people breaking in once he'd doctored up those two bottles.

Now that I've given you the background perhaps you will be able to better appreciate what happened when another so-called doctor came to town one August afternoon. He was one of the medicine men who traveled the back roads of our country in the early years of this century selling their nostrums to the unwary.

To make sure everyone in town knew that he had arrived, "Doctor Gazain" drove his horse and carriage up and down our hill street twice. The carriage looked like a small enclosed stage coach except that the driver did not sit on top but steered his horse with reins that went through a window above the dashboard. Along its roofline was a cloth banner bearing the words; "Dr. Gazain, Pawnee Medicine Man. Come!" At the post office and on the town hall bulletin boards, he had posted further information. Dr. Gazain would do a magic show and present stereoptican lantern slides and acquaint us with the powerful medicines of the Pawnee Indians and Siam. At the depot! Seven o'clock sharp. Everybody welcome. No charge.

Half the townspeople (including me) had gathered in front of the medicine man's stage coach before he opened its door. Standing behind a table he'd set up there, suddenly he lifted both arms in the air and spoke in a loud, vibrant voice. "My friends, I am Dr. White Cloud Gazain whose mission in life, my friends, is to bring joy and relief from suffering to the people of this land. First, let us have a bit of the joy!" From the back of the table which was covered by a bright red and yellow cloth he brought forth a gold trumpet and played The Darktown Strutter's Ball. He was good! As the lively clear notes echoed throughout the valley we were tapping our feet. When he finished everyone clapped.

"I thank you, my friends," the medicine man said, "but you do me too much honor. My trumpet does not seem to be working right. Let me see!" He reached into the bell of the horn. "Ah," he said. "So that's what's wrong!" Then he pulled out of that trumpet yards and yards of purple ribbon. It was magic for sure. No horn could possibly hold all that ribbon. The applause was universal. Dr. Gazain waited for it to subside.

"Tell you what I'm gonna do," he said. "First I'm gonna tell you how I learned the ancient salubrious medical secrets of the Pawnee Indians and those known only to the king of Siam. Then, I shall mystify and entertain you with more magic, because happiness, my friends, is man's best medicine. Then, my friends, I may, if you are worthy, bring out from my chariot some bottles of elixir from the Root of the Royal Banyan Tree. Finally, and again only if you are worthy, I will conclude the program with lantern slides of the wonders of the world, including Niagra Falls in all its cascading glory. I will not take up a collection, my friends. I am here to educate and heal poor mortals whose miseries are not those of their own making. Will you be worthy?" We sure resolved to be, and to stay there till we'd seen Niagra Falls.

I can't remember his exact words but Dr. Gazain told us in an almost hypnotic voice he'd been abandoned as an orphan, some kind Pawnee Indians had taken him in, that their medicine man shaman had adopted him as his own son and had taught him all the secret Indian lore about the healing properties of herbs, roots, and other wild things, secrets that he said modern medicine had not yet discovered.

As for Siam, Dr. Gazain said he'd been a sailor in his youth and young manhood, "I tell you, my friends, that in that time I sailed the seven seas and was shipwrecked thrice." The last time was off the coast of Siam, he said, and he barely made it to shore with the sharks pursuing him. Sure made us shudder, the way he told it. Now, seventy years later I can't remember exactly how he said he made it to the court of the King of Siam but I do know that he said he'd cured that king of sciatica and rheumatism and the bloody thrush by using the knowledge he'd learned from the Pawnee shaman.

"My friends," he roared. "I wish you could have been there when they honored me. Thousands of Siamese, many of them twins, sitting on those marble steps, all chanting the words of the national song of Siam: Owah, tana Siam; Jeewa tana Siam. It was only later when I said the words of the song of Siam swiftly that I realized that Dr. Gazain had a fine sense of humor. "And the King made me many presents, he did, and he ordered his physicians to impart to me all the medical wisdom they possessed. Among those presents, my friends, was a chunk of the Root of the Royal Banyan Tree. There's only one tree like it in the whole world," the medicine man said. He claimed that he alone had the only root of it and the knowledge and formula for distilling it, and that was why he felt called to share that marvelous medication with poor folk who needed it. I know it sounds fraudulent as hell but there in the valley as the sun went down, the medicine man in his top hat and long frock coat had us almost hypnotized.

To capture the few unbelievers, Dr. Gazain then took off his top hat, showed us it was empty, then placed it top down on the table before him. "Abracadabra!" he intoned twice, then reached into the hat and pulled out a white rabbit. It was a live one too, big as a snowshoe hare, and it kicked feebly before the medicine man put it down in a basket by the table. Oh how we clapped! Later I suspected that his hat had a hinged top and he pulled the rabbit through a slit in the table cover from a box beneath it, but I don't know.

Next the medicine man brought out a case of bottles from under the table and made his spiel, offering a free bottle of elixer from the Root of the Royal Banyan Tree to the first person to come forward. Lord, there was a real rush of people but Charley Olafson got the free one. The medicine man said he wasn't selling the elixer, wouldn't take a cent for it, but would accept two dollars a bottle from anyone as a contribution so that he could continue his good work all over the U.P. Dr. Gazain never stopped talking as he took in the money and handed over the bottles of elixer. It would cure not only sciatica and rheumatism; it would also free one from headaches, rashes, menstrual cramps, and a hundred other ailments.

119

When finally the selling spree tapered off, the medicine man brought out an ointment made from herbs known only to the Pawnee Indians, good for both man and beast he said. It would cure horses' spavins, reduce bloat in cows, and could completely eradicate sore shoulders and backs in man. Then he sold Pawnee soap guaranteed to eliminate blackheads and improve the complexion. Our people sure forked over their money. Even if the stuff didn't work, it was reasonably priced. When Dr. Gazain saw that most of the fleece had been sheared he played again on his trumpet, this time "Marching Through Georgia." It was time for the lantern show because it was almost dark. The medicine man draped a white sheet over his coach and set up his lantern on the table, poured a bit of water in the reservoir and pumped it until you could smell the fumes of carbide. Then he lit the carbide lamp, adjusted the lenses, and put in the first slide. The picture on the screen was dim by modern standards but it was recognizable. It showed the Rocky Mountains and the medicine man gave us a short lecture about them. Then he showed a bridge over the Mississippi River, the largest, longest river in the world, he said. "You good people of Tioga should be proud! The waters from your river and lake are one of the sources of this mighty river!" We cheered when he told us that.

The next slide he showed us was a picture of the royal temples of Siam. With a pointer he showed us about where the king's palace had been when he was there. There were so many spires and onion-like steeples we couldn't quite make out the palace but we took the medicine man's word for it.

Finally the climax, Niagra Falls! All of us had heard of its majesty and a few had seen small pictures of it but here on the projection screen it must have been four feet tall. You could almost hear the roar of it. When Dr. Gazain bade us all goodnight, saying that he'd stay with us another day and hold another magic show the next evening, a lot of our people resolved to raid their sugar bowls for enough raha money to buy more medicine before he wandered on.

Having heard my report about the magic show and the medicine man's success in selling all his stuff, my father was there in the front row that next evening. You could see people nudging each other when they noted his presence. Dr. Gazain followed much the same procedure he'd used the evening before but he had some new magic tricks and some new tunes on his trumpet. Two of the tricks I remember. In the first one, he pulled out a big scarf, folded it and with some large scissors cut it in two. Then with a flourish and some incantations, he unfolded it to show a complete, uncut scarf. In the other trick, he had our village blacksmith tie his hands tightly together behind his back with a rope. He then went into his coach and came out completely untied, yet with the rope all in one piece. Our blacksmith, Patrick Feeny, said later that he'd tied the knots so tightly

120

no one could have untied them in so short a time.

Unfortunately for the medicine man, his sales of the esoteric medicines and ointments that second evening were almost zero. Our people, conscious of Dad's presence, weren't going to take the chance of insulting him by buying any. They knew that the medicine man would soon be traveling on and that they'd need their doctor many times. They enjoyed the show and the tunes and the spiels but only Pete LaCosse bought anything. It was a jar of ointment, and Pete came over to tell my dad that it was for his horse, not for him.

The next morning, the medicine man drove up to our door and knocked. Dad received him amicably and asked him what he wanted. Dr. Gazain said that he was almost out of medicine bottles and wanted to buy three dozen if my father could spare them.

As my father told the tale later, he enjoyed the conversation very much. "I like a fraud that knows he's a fraud," he said. "He told me his elixer was a concoction of swamp water, alcohol, burnt sugar for coloring, and Angustora bitters to make it taste bad, that he knew it wouldn't hurt anyone but that, as one professional to another, it seemed to help a lot of people.

"Then we got to talking about magic," Dad said. "He's a pretty good magician and he sure liked my belt trick which he solved right away. Said he'd put it in his act. And when I asked him to show me how he did that cutting of the scarf yet had it unfold to be a complete one, he showed me how. So I sold him thirty bottles and told him to say Hi! to the King of Siam."

THE TAMING OF TIM O'LEARY

As the Sultan of Suju remarked when he declined an invitation to go to a horse race held in his honor, "It has already been my observation that one horse can run faster than another," so too it has been my observation that there are two kinds of Irish, the red and the black, which, when mixed together, will always give birth to a fine explosion.

In Tioga there were only a few handfuls of Irish left after the mines shut down. Of them Mollie Malone was the prettiest - which is saying a lot. Her hair was as black as the ravens that croaked over our hills all winter, yet she had eyes of a startlingly clear blue. Having come to Tioga straight from the Ould Sod to be the mining superintendent's hired girl, her complexion still had the shine of County Kerry in it. A good worker too, Henry Thompson said, but he just wished she were uglier. All the young bucks in the village, no matter what their nationality, were after Mollie Malone.

Tim O'Leary was after her too and Mollie liked that, she did. He was red Irish with flaming hair on the head of him, and on his legs, huge arms, and chest. A big man, a strong man, and a wild man,

Tim O'Leary was convinced that life was his personal orange, and, by the grace of St. Bridget, he'd suck every bit of juice out of it. Unlike Mollie, Tim had been born in this country, indeed in Tioga, because his father, Malachi O'Leary had built a cabin by the depot after having helped build the railroad into town.

Many of his teachers often wished that Tim had been born elsewhere for the boy was a bundle of constant devilment, bright enough but so full of energy and restlessness he just couldn't help but raise hell. When he left school after the eighth grade, things sure calmed down and the teachers could stop biting their nails.

By the time he was twenty-one, Tim O'Leary had done all the things in Tioga that were doable and screwed all the girls who were screwable so he caught a freight going south and was gone over a year. All he ever said about it was that he'd sure seen a lot of country but none that was as good as the U.P. By the time he returned Malachi O'Leary and his mother were dead so he moved into the old cabin, planning to start in where he'd left off. He got a job immediately with Silverthorne and Company who were logging the back country northwest of Lake Tioga serving as a skidder, then sawyer, and in two years, straw woods boss. Made good money and when he came to town Tim spent it, but somehow things weren't quite the same. His old pursuits just didn't seem to have the old fine flavor of hellishness.

That was when he met Mollie Malone. With one of the Thompson kids on her lap, she was swinging on a little board seat hung by ropes from a tall tree limb. Tim saw her legs first, a lot of them, as the swing made its arc. Wow! And then her figure, and then her hair, and eyes, and then her legs again. Ever brash and unafraid, Tim leaped the fence and began pushing the two of them higher and higher. The view from underneath was better that way. "Stop it, ye fule or ye'll be the death av both of us," Mollie yelled. When he slowed down the ropes and held them still, she gave him a bit of her mind, she did. "Glory be!" he thought, "from the sound of her there's some Irish here." He was contrite as he introduced himself. "Oh," said she, "So here's the wild Irishman they've be a-telling me about. A no-good son of Satan, they said. Well good day to you, spalpeen, and may our paths never cross in the bog again." She took the Thompson kid into the house and didn't even give her name. Tim hardly knew what she'd been saying. All he could hear was that rich Irish brogue with its rolled r's and the lilt of it, and the low musical voice that twanged the Irish harp in him.

Well, that was how the courtship of Mollie Malone began. No stormier one had ever waggled so many Tioga tongues. In April Tim walked up the hill with a huge bouquet of arbutus in one hand and a fist in the other, daring anyone he met to make some crack about them. No one did. When he knocked at the back door of the Thompson house and held the arbutus out to her without a word, she threw them in his face. In May he did the same with blue flags, the lovely wild iris that grows in the swamps near Tioga. Mollie told him never to do it again but she took them. He bought her a box of chocolate creams that had been on the shelf of Flinn's store for five years and she never told him they were inedible. Renting a horse and buggy from Marchand on a fine June Sunday (Mollie had Sundays off), he drove her down to Lake Tioga and then up the river road that tunneled through the forest. She only slapped his face hard three times, and softly twice.

On a hot Sunday afternoon in July they walked the trail down to Lake Tioga and had a picnic on the little rock point where Beaverdam Creek enters the lake. It's a nice spot with a patch of moss and plenty of stones to skip in the water. "Sure hot, Mollie," Tim said. "Let's go swimming." She gave him the look. "Do ye think now that Mollie Malone is another of the wenches ye've had under a bush? I'll have you know, Mister O'Leary, of the bog Irish O'Learys, that I'm a decent woman, I am...." She was just warming up her tongue to give him more fits when suddenly, on an impulse, the wild Irishman stripped to his red hairy hide and jumped in the lake. Mollie did not cover her eyes. She took his shoes and flung them far out in the lake; she took his clothes and did the same, then ran up the trail home, giggling. He couldn't catch up to her, running across all those stones in his naked feet.

All Tioga knew that Tim O'Leary and Mollie Malone once had a fight down at the post office when she had gone there to buy a stamp for a letter going to Ireland. She was peering through the wall of postal boxes trying to see if Annie, the postmistress, was there when Tim appeared. Annie wasn't there. She'd gone out of the back door because she had the trots. The whole town knew that Annie never could eat cabbage; it always did that to her. Well, Tim tried to help Mollie see if Annie was there by grabbing her legs and lifting her up above his head so she could see over the partition. Wow, was Mollie mad! The people who were there said she scratched his face with her fingernails till the blood came, and beat hard on the big man's chest with her little fists, all the while giving tongue. Trying to look contrite, Tim apologized for his impulsive behavior but he remembered the feel of those lovely legs well enough to bear the next three weeks of rejection.

By August month they were seeing each other a lot, and fighting together a lot, as the black and red Irish are prone to do. Rarely did Tim take a nip or two or three at Higley's as had been his custom. The boys who played poker in the backroom of Callahan's store missed his wild humor and his money. He didn't even go trout fishing any more. All Tim O'Leary had in his wild Irish head was that black haired colleen with the blue eyes. Yes, he had it bad, he did. When occasionally she called him "Timmy" the strength of him melted away.

Oh how the two of them argued and fought! Once, when he was trying to be honest with her, Tim had said he was not the marrying kind, that he didn't want anything running around his house but a sidewalk, and she should be warned thereby. He never did hear the last of that. Mollie Malone made it very clear that *she* would be married someday and would have children, lots of them. She told him to leave her alone until that man who could be a father came along. The very thought of that other man filled Tim with fury. He wished he hadn't told her of his wild need for freedom, of his fear of being trapped.

One afternoon when they were lying on the moss at the point where she'd thrown his clothes and shoes into the lake, the fire in Tim O'Leary's pants flared with desire so strongly he couldn't help pulling Mollie's skirt up to her waist. Before he could do anything, however, she picked up a rock and, holding it in her hand, hit him in the temple with it so hard she knocked him unconscious. As he regained his senses, Tim found Mollie keening over him, her black hair on his face, kissing him passionately. As long as he lived, Tim O'Leary never forgot that moment - or the rock.

Shortly after that Tim offered to go to Mass with Mollie. She showed her joy if not her triumph at the thought but she refused. "Not until, as a good Catholic, ye've gone to confession," she said. "You've a bundle of sins to account for, Timmy, and Mollie Malone is not to forgive them unless the Lord can."

The thought of going to confession appalled the Irishman. How much should he tell? What would be the penances? Feeling his freedom slipping and angry with the whole business, he decided to flee. He'd take the train for Milwaukee, then Minneapolis and head west. To hell with Mollie Malone and confession and marriage and everything else. A man's life was his own, it was. But when he got to the depot he couldn't buy the ticket.

So Tim O'Leary went to confession. And so they got married. And, despite the rhythm method, ten months later Mollie Malone gave birth to a ten pound little devil with a mass of red hair. And they fought happily ever after!

CLOTHESLINES

o account of the old days in the Upper Peninsula of Michigan would be complete without some mention of the role of the hired girl. Now, she has disappeared along with the buckboards, cutters, and the surreys (with or without fringes) of that time, but during the first third of this century almost any family that could afford from thirty to sixty dollars a month in wages employed one. The hired girl was not a servant nor did she regard herself as such. She was a household-aid in the same sense that we have nurses-aids today. She did a lot of the dirty work, the hard work, around the house, the washing, ironing, churning and cleaning but she rarely did these alone. The woman of the house shared these duties with her if only to make sure they were done right. Occasionally, the hired girl even did some of the cooking and baking but only if she were deemed worthy after careful training.

Back then there were few opportunities for a young girl to earn any money at all. Boys could trap for furs, do chores, and later cut pulpwood, but only by picking berries and selling them could a girl get a few coins for her buckskin purse. Accordingly, a position as hired girl was eagerly sought for. Not only did the meager wages seem huge, but they were also steady and, besides, just being in a comparatively wealthy home was an education in itself. Hired girls didn't eat in the kitchen; they ate with us even when company came. They became members of the family.

The Gage household had a whole procession of hired girls when I was a child and a boy. Most of them stayed only a year or two until they had saved up enough to take the train for Milwaukee, Chicago or Detroit, or to get married. My mother always felt a real obligation to make sure that each of them benefited from their stay with us. She taught them how a fine, loving home was run; she taught them manners; she bought them clothing and taught them how to be attractive. One of them she even taught to play the piano. When inevitably, they left our home, they did so with regret for they knew how much the experience had changed them for the better.

I only remember a few of our hired girls. There was Nana, a tall Finn girl who used to scare the liver and lights out of me with Finnish folk lore. Though more than seventy years have passed I still shiver recalling her tales of descending the ladder into hell with new evil monsters at every level. And there was the pretty French-Canadian girl, Marie, full of love and mischievous gaiety, who taught me, complete with translation, some lively and bawdy French songs. Dad had to fire her after she and the delivery man were discovered screwing in our woodshed. Then there was Thelma, a gawky Finn girl from a very poor home way out in the country who slept in one of our back bedrooms and went home each weekend. She was fired too when our house began to swarm with the bedbugs she brought to us. Lord, how those bedbugs could bite! Red hot needles, they were. It took Mother two weeks of frantic work until they were gone.

The best of our hired girls was Siiri Arvilla. Dad found her slaving in the kitchen of a lumber camp doing all the cooking for twenty men. She was a tiny little thing, only thirteen at the time, just skin and bones, and worn to a frazzle by the hard labor. Well, Dad couldn't bear it so Siiri came to our house, first only to help Mother with the dishes, but later to rule the entire roost. Siiri was a local girl, the oldest of six children, and she'd had to leave school in the sixth grade to help take care of them and earn money to help support the family. But she was extremely intelligent and so hungry to learn she mastered almost all my mother could teach her in the first year with us.

We loved Siiri and she loved us. I always thought of her as a sister. After she fattened up and felt secure with us she really blossomed as a real member of our family. When she laughed, the whole house rocked with merriment. She seemed to know everything that ever happened in town and kept us informed with a wit and choice of colorful language that never failed to entrance us. Why we even liked to help her do the dishes just to hear her talk. I think I caught my need to tell short and tall tales from Siiri for she was not averse to doing a little exaggerating now and then if it made the story better. It wasn't that she lied when she told us the details of the first bath old Eric Niemi had ever known; it was more like what Poobah in The

127

Mikado described when he was accused of falsehood. "It is no lie," said Poohbah. "It is merely corroborative detail intended to give artistic verisimilitude to a bald and unconvincing narrative." Phew, that's a mouthful!

Siiri soon proved to be indispensible. As Mother's health failed, she took over. She planned the meals, ordered the groceries, told my father when he needed a haircut or a new suit, coddled and entertained my mother, and served as our confidant. When my sister fell in love with a handsome French Canadian boy of whom Dad didn't approve, Siiri served as the passer of notes between them. When Dad was out on his medical rounds Siiri answered the phone, took down the symptoms of the patient, then told Dad what the diagnosis was. Dad said he'd never had a better nurse in an emergency, that she could take out stitches better than he could.

All of us kept out of the kitchen on Monday mornings and Saturday afternoons. That was Siiri's law! On Saturday afternoon she washed her brown hair (which hung to her waist when uncoiled) then put it up in braids around her head. Siiri always kicked up her heels dancing on Saturday night. Monday was wash and pasty day and she wasn't going to be bothered by any interruptions then either. Stay out of the kitchen! After building a hot fire in the wood range she filled the big copper boiler with water from the rain barrel, shaved the cakes of brown soap to dissolve in a sauce pan, then got out the bleach and the wooden stirring stick. Next, Siiri made the pasties with their onions, rutabagas and a touch of kidney to go with the meat and potatoes inside that tasty crust. Many people from Down Below have never had the privilege of biting into a genuine U.P. pasty smeared with ketchup and with a dill pickle on the side. They are the deprived unfortunates of this earth. May they at least go to heaven after they die!

While the pasties were baking, Siiri boiled the clothes, scrubbed them on the blue corrugated washboard, rinsed them, put them through the wringer and sometimes boiled and rinsed them again. She did this whole sequence not just once but two or three times, depending on how many dirty clothes were in the pile by the stove. Washing was hard work there in the steamy kitchen of long ago but Siiri did it with pride. "It's all worth it," she said, "once you get them on the line a-flapping in the wind." Siiri claimed she really enjoyed it when Dad bought her a manually operated washing machine, then, after electricity came to Tioga in 1919, an electric one. My father, having starved his way through medical school, was pretty tight with a dollar or a dime but anything Siiri wanted, she got. He even bought her an electric mangle so she could put away the sad irons or use them as door stops.

I used to enjoy seeing Siiri hang up the clothes. We had two long lines in the side yard and a clothes reel, the latter an elevated platform with a post on one end that supported revolving vanes strung with wire. Siiri usually filled the clothes reel first. She'd stand back for a few minutes thinking, then start creating her weekly art form, often dipping first into one basket then into the others for just the right piece to fill out her plan. Siiri liked symmetry but was not bound to it completely. She liked to contrast colors and sizes. I remember her once asking me to be sure to wear and dirty up a yellow shirt I had so it would look pretty on her next clothesline pattern.

Never did Siiri hang the clothes as they came out of basket. She left gaps which she later filled with just the right item. Some people paint, some sculp; Siiri's art form was her clothesline. She could make that clothes reel look like a huge bouquet and her long lines just made you feel good to look at the garments fluttering with color in the wind.

But clotheslines filled with flapping laundry were not merely an art form to Siiri; they were also her weekly newspaper as I discovered late one Monday afternooon when I walked home with her. It was an education. She examined carefully every clothesline at every house to provide me with an interpretive commentary. "Oh, see Cully. Sam's been poaching again. Shot a deer, probably by shining it with his carbide lantern after dark." All I saw were some clothes dangling from the line.

"Yes. See his long underwear, Cully? Its right sleeve still has a red brown stain at the elbow. That's a blood stain, awfully hard to get out. His shirt's all right so he probably took that off before he cleaned the deer but didn't roll up the sleeves of his underwear far enough when he reached way up in the chest cavity to cut the windpipe so he could get the lungs out. If he'd done it by daylight he'd seen that the blood would get on them." Made sense.

At the next house Siiri said, "They've sure been having a hard time. Not enough money. Look at that patched tablecloth. It's done neat enough but no woman would put a patched tablecloth on her table. Patched pants, sure. Yes, see her husbands overalls? They've got patches on the patches at the knee. Hope he gets a job soon. See, he's made her home-made clothespins out of maple branches."

So it went, all the way up the street. Even the absence of clothing meant something to Siiri's keen eye. No night shirts or night gowns? They probably sleep together naked at night. An empty line? "The woman's been ailing for some time and may be really sick. I'll have to tell Doctor. He'll go see her."

Two lines full of heavy men's clothing? Siiri knew why. "They've finished cutting pine at the headwaters of Dishno Creek and Pete's come back home at last from the camp bringing all his stuff with him. I bet the first thing he did was go sauna."

A pretty new highly embroidered head shawl? "That's Mrs. Piirto's Sunday huivija. I guess she's finally made up her mind to go to church again. Stopped going when her little daughter died a year ago. She's healing , and that's good."

Two sheets still grey? Siiri was contemptuous. "A lazy woman, she is. I'd be ashamed to put a sheet that looked like that on my line. Must be the Indian blood in her, she being French Canadian. Even if she'd run out of bleach she could have put wood ashes in the water and boiled them again."

She was more tolerant at the next house where a string of assorted socks, many of them with holes showing, hung on the line. "It's her arthritis," Siiri said. "Poor old lady, her hands are so crippled she can hardly hold a needle."

At another old lady's house, Mrs. Beatty's, the only thing that hung on the line was a man's shirt. Siiri began to laugh. "So Ed Beatty's heading back to California," she commented. "The delivery-man told me he'd had it with his mother even if this was the first time he'd come back in twenty years. Seems that she still thinks of him as her baby and the other night she was hovering over him when he was asleep and dropped the lamp chimney right on his bald head."

Another line with a white (rather than flannel) man's shirt? "John must have gone to his brother's funeral. Heard tell he died last Thursday."

Thirteen diapers? "Oh that poor little tyke has got diarrhea again. Doctor says he can't figure out why. I told your father their well was a shallow one and maybe they'd better start boiling their drinking water or go get some from the spring."

Slightly pink dish towels? "Will that woman ever learn to put the red flannel shirts in last, after all the white stuff is out of the boiler? She's plain dumb. Always has been. Why he married her, I don't know. Maybe it was because his own mother was sharp as a tack and too bossy."

Slightly pink bags made of cheesecloth? "You can't find a better jelly maker in town than Minnie, or a better baker, except probably me. I'll go visit her this afternoon on my way back to your house so she'll give me a bite of bread with that wild strawberry jelly on it."

Heavy blankets with little holes in them? "Moths!" said Siiri. "Washing won't help. They'll come again. What she needs to do is pack them in a drawer with a lot of new cedar shavings. Even if her husband doesn't have a plane, he could whittle some for her. But they've been fighting each other a long time."

New bib overalls, two pair of them? "Oh good, Eino finally sold that forty acres of spruce he's been trying to get rid of but Sandra will have to wash them again before they'll be fit to wear. Always stiff as a board when new."

Siiri's face softened at the next house. "Oh look, Cully. Grand-children coming." There were baby blankets and small quilts hanging on the line.

130

When we came to Widow Untilla's house, Siiri was puzzled. "That's funny," she said. "Why did she hang all those sheets on the front line rather than the back one where she always put them?" Unable to resist, Siiri moved over to get a better look and came back snickering. "Why that damned old goat!" she exclaimed. "Cheating again. I know that's Erkki Niemi's long underwear. I've seen it hanging on Mrs. Niemi's line often. There's a hole in the left knee. Hmm! Making sure he could make a fast getaway if he had to. Erkki probably screwed Widow Untilla with his shoes and underwear on and knowing his wife would be sure to feel the crust or smell it - he had the widow wash them. And, it being his only pair, he's probably going around without any on. But if so his wife would wonder where it was when she went to bed with him. I bet he went to his camp for a few days."

Just then we met Mrs. Untilla on her way to Flinn's store, and after a few pleasantries Siiri asked her how her husband was, that she hadn't seen him around recently. "Oh, he's gone to his shack for a few days," Mrs. Untilla replied. "Hope he brings back some trout."

Siiri married her husband when she was forty. It made no difference. She managed two households as well as she had ours. Before she died, she arranged it so that my father who lived to be ninety four was well taken care of for the rest of his days. People called her our hired girl but none of our family did. She was Siiri, one of the finest persons I've ever known.

HOOKY

**N**ever had there been such a fine May day! It was warm - in the upper seventies with a blue sky and sun - so warm that Miss Polson had opened the classroom windows. Birds were singing out there; dogs were romping around out there; grass for bare feet was growing out there, and all of us boys had itches in our breeches. Oh to run free, to say to hell with school. Eleven more days of it. No, eleven more years! We'd never get out of jail. I hardly heard Miss Polson's voice asking me to tell about Peru until her sharp crack of her ruler opened my mind and ears.

"Peru is a country in South America," I recited as if in a dream. "It is a mountainous country bounded on the north by Ecuador and Brazil, on the east and south by Columbia, Argentina and Chile. Its capital is Lima. It exports minerals..." I'd memorized the damned stuff and it just leaked out of my mouth though I didn't know what I was saying. I just wasn't there. I was on top of a hill lying in tall grass, watching white clouds go by. And I was still on the hill when Miss Polson said, "That is satisfactory, Cully," and mercifully diverted her attention to another classmate.

Recess was too short. It was always too short but this time someone surely must have rung the bell too soon. Nevertheless Mullu, Fisheye, Sulu and I had managed to make plans to play hooky that afternoon.

After our noon meal we'd start on the way to school but sneak off past the Lutheran church and meet by Sliding Rock, then we'd go to Fish Lake to fish and swim or do anything else that we felt like doing. "Remember to put a hook and some worms in your pocket," Mullu said.

The decision to play hooky was not lightly undertaken. We knew we would pay for it dearly. For me it meant not one whipping but two. The first, and I knew it would be the worst, would come from Old Blue Balls, our tough school superintendent, the second from my father after I got home. Mullu would probably get two like I would because his little brother would be sure to squeal on him but his mother would do the spanking. Maybe Sulu would escape the home punishment unless someone tattled. Fisheye would only get one spanking because his folks didn't really care what happened to him, the oldest of their nine children. He wandered free and slept in the hay mow at night. We often envied Fisheye almost as much as he envied us.

Yes, our decision to play hooky that afternoon was a measure of our desperate need to escape the close confines of the classroom walls and Miss Polson's harsh discipline. We knew what we'd have coming to us. Old Blue Balls had made it very clear. He visited every schoolroom, shot blue fire at us from his eye, and told us that there would be no unexcused absences, that any truant would have his hide tanned. We knew he meant it too.

Mr. Donegal - that was his real name - ran his school with an iron hand. Teachers and pupils alike were terrified of him and with good reason. He had a repertoire of three punishments, the hardwood ruler, The Hand, and the razor strap in order of severity. I'd just had the ruler across the wrists and that was bad enough but Mullu, Sulu and Fisheye had experienced all three. They often argued about whether The Hand or the strap were the worst. Sulu was for The Hand. He said that he'd been sore for two weeks after he'd unknowingly made the mistake of clobbering Old Blue Ball's bare hind end, thinking it was Emil in the other booth of the outhouse. Fisheye said either the razor strap or The Hand could hurt the most, depending upon Old Blue Ball's mood of the moment. He'd had so many beatings, both at home and at school, he knew he could handle one more. What the hell! It was spring. Let's go!

All our fears were wiped out once we started down the little path to Fish Lake. Instead we had that delicious feeling of carefree devilment, knowing we were doing something bad but not giving a damn. We raced each other in spurts; we jumped up and down like springer spaniels; Sulu made handsprings. When we came to the little creek that we had to cross on a narrow ten foot log Mullu dared us to do it hopping on one foot but when he led the way and fell off we laughed ourselves sick and crossed pigeon-toed the way we always did. Where the trail crosses swamp we found a big frog and finally corraled it. "Good pike bait!" said Fisheye as he stuffed it, wrapped in a handful of moss, into his pocket. Finally we got to the lake.

I've got to describe the lake so you can understand what happened. Fish Lake wasn't a big lake, as lakes in the U.P. go. I'd judge it to be maybe a mile long and a half mile wide. Lined with spruce, balsam and white birch, it always seemed to me to be about to brim over, the way the clear water rippled under the Labrador tea bushes at its edge. At Big Rock, where the trail ended in a little clearing filled with the debris of old campfires, a granite cliff sloped and then plunged into deep water but there were little cracks and ledges along its incline where you could sit and fish. Just offshore, about thirty yards away, was a little island covered with blueberry bushes and a few tamaracks. No Tioga kid ever thought he could swim until he managed to make it to that island and back. Seventy years later I still remember my triumph and terror when, for the first time, I swam across the deep channel.

Big Rock was on a point that ran out into the lake and on both sides of it were little bays lined with lilypads. On the further edge of the east bay was The Log where the slippery carcuss of a huge old white pine jutted far into the water. A little spring creek entered the lake beside The Log, so it was always a fine place to fish. The east bay, to the right of Big Rock and the island, was larger, ending at Boat Rock. I don't know why they called it that for we never saw a boat on Fish Lake when I was a boy.

First the four of us went fishing. In our pockets, each of us, except Mullu, had a cedar bobber wrapped with braided black line and a few hooks squeezed into a scrap of tinfoil. I uncoiled my line, cut it with my jacknife, and gave half to Mullu who whittled and peeled a bobber from a dry stick at one of the old campfires. Then we cut "government poles" from alder branches, wrapped the tips with the line, put on the hooks and bobbers and were ready to go. Fisheye said he'd try for pike with his frog so he and Sulu fished off a ledge in the deep water there at Big Rock while Mullu and I followed the path along the bay to The Log. All of us had our shoes off by that time and were reveling in the freedom of our wiggled toes. Besides, on that slippery rock or on The Log, bare feet could get a better grip than the hard soles of our school shoes.

Mullu had hard luck. The first fish he caught from way out on the end of the log was a big perch but it dropped off as he made his way back to shore. Then he caught a big ugly bullhead that had swallowed the hook so far down he had to spend a lot of time trying to get it out, getting horned by the fish in the process. Bullheads are nasty fish that way. I never tried to take the hook out of any I caught. Just nailed it to a tree and cut its head off with the hook still in it. You get horned by a bullhead and you've got a sore hand for a long time.

I was luckier. I knew by the way the bobber acted I had a trout on the line and it was, a fat nine incher whose beautiful spots shone in the sun. I cleaned it right away and laid it on some moss by the path. Then I caught a chub which I threw away before remembering that I might use it off Big Rock for pike. Then, after a lot of little nibbles that just fluttered the bobber I pulled out a big sucker. It would be all right to eat. Early in the spring, sucker meat is still firm and sweet, not soft and muddy tasting as it gets in summertime. Last of all I caught a seven inch perch and since all of the worms in my pocket were gone, carrying the fish on a forked maple branch, I went back to the other kids at Big Rock.

Fisheye hadn't had a hit. His frog, hooked through the lips, was just floating in the water, occasionally giving a lazy twitch. Sulu had three perch. Well, that was enough. We'd have ourselves a fish fry. Sulu had even brought some salt in a folded paper, he said. So we gathered a lot of dry maple branches from the edge of the clearing along with some birch bark and started a fire.

There was some debate about how we should cook the fish. Mullu suggested skewering them on a peeled branch of hard maple and toasting them over the flames. "No," said Sulu, "All we'll get that way is burned skin and raw meat. We've got to have coals, not flames, no matter what we do. The best way is to wrap the fish in clay and lay them on the coals to bake."

Fisheye heard the argument and said that he knew there was a clay bank up in the woods where an old yellow birch had toppled over. He'd go get some clay, he said, if we would watch his pole which he had propped up in a crevice surrounded by some rocks. But as he began to climb up the granite suddenly there was a big splash and the frog, line and pole were cleaving through the water heading for Boat Rock. Oh how we groaned. That was a BIG pike! Oh well, we had enough fish anyway.

As the big fire burned down, with the clay clumps of fish beside it, we just lay there in the sunshine happier than we'd been in a long time. "This is the life!" exclaimed Sulu. "If I can ever get old enough to quit school I'm going to do nothing but fish until I die." The mention of school kind of put a damper on things for a moment but we soon forgot. Too nice a day to think of school or old Blue Balls. We talked a little about what we'd do when we grew up. Fisheye said he was going to Alaska and mine for gold. Mullu hoped to get a job on one of the big whale-back ore boats he'd seen in the harbor at Marquette. Sulu might become a trapper, he said. I didn't know what I was going to do or be and at that moment didn't care. It was enough just to be there in the sunshine with a soft breeze blowing through my toes. But mostly we didn't talk at all; it was enough just being a boy there on Big Rock on a fine spring afternoon.

The fish weren't too bad after cooking on the coals for about an hour but of course thirteen and fourteen year old boys will eat anything. When the clay shells were removed, the fish skins went with them, so we put on some of Sulu's salt and ate them with relish and plenty of ashes and dirt. Then Fisheye threw off his clothes and dived into the lake. "Last one in is a sissy!" he yelled, so of course all the rest of us joined him. Oooh that water was cold! We jumped in, threshed around and came back to the fire as quick as we could. Then we jumped in again, and again. Oh how good it felt to be naked, free from every constraint!

"Let's swim out to the island," Fisheye proposed once we got used to the cold water. I was a bit dubious but went along with the others. We were prancing up and down on the island's little sandy beach to get warm enough for the swim back when suddenly we heard a roar. "Boys! Boys! Come here!" It was old Blue Balls himself right there by our clothes and the fire.

What to do? We held a conference. Perhaps if one of us swam over to Boat Rock or The Log, Blue Balls would follow that one and the rest of us could get our clothes and run. No, that was too far to swim in that cold water.

"Mullu! Cully! Sulu! Fisheye!" Old Blue Balls knew who we were. "Come back here or I'll skin the hides off you! Quick!

There was nothing to do but swim back though we did it slowly. Even so, I got there first and clung to the rock unable to bring myself to climb up to where he was.

Then I heard Sulu yell for help. "I can't move my legs!" he cried, and turning, I could see that his body was doubled up in the water and he was flailing it with his arms. I knew what had happened. He'd developed a cramp and it had hit his legs first. Soon it would go to his arms and that would be it!

As I thought of turning and trying to go to help Sulu, suddenly Old Blue Balls came charging down the rock. Flinging off his coat as he did so, he jumped into the lake and swam arm over arm as fast as he could to grab the drowning boy. He missed Sulu the first time but got him the second and swimming sidearm, brought him to shore. Sulu sure looked bad.

A lot of things happend in the next few minutes. Old Blue Balls swatted Sulu on the back, sat down on a log, and rolled him back and forth across his knees, then pushed at his belly. Holding him over his shoulder, he scattered our fire to one side with his feet, then laid Sulu down on the hot ground where the fire had been. Old Blue Balls then grabbed all our clothes and piled them over Sulu. "Boys! Get some fresh dry wood and build up the fires on each side. He's so cold, he's blue, and I'm afraid he'll stop breathing. Hurry now!" Boy, did we hurry!

Only when some color came back to Sulu's face and lips, did Blue Balls realize how wet he was. Soaked to the hide, he took everything off him, wringing each article as he did so, until he was as naked as we were. Wow! What a man! He was covered with brown hair all over but what transfixed us was the sight of his balls. They weren't blue at all. They were huge and hung low but they were just the color of his hair. As he saw us looking, a wide grin came over his face. It was the first time we'd ever seen him smile. "Well, boys," he said at last, "I guess you know you've been calling me wrong all the time, eh? That sure froze us. "Yes, Mr. Donegal. No, Mr. Donegal." Now we were going to get it.

But Mr. Donegal uncovered Sulu and held him in his arms a moment as he listened to his heart and breathing. "Well boys," he said, "I guess Sulu's cooked so let's put on our clothes and go home." He helped Sulu dress before he put on his own clothes and on the way back along the path he picked Sulu up and carried him a spell.

Somehow it seemed like a very long way home and, as we trudged along following him. I kept thinking of those brown balls and singing to myself one of the bawdy songs my Grandpa Gage had taught me. The tune was one of Sousa's marches - perhaps the Stars and Stripes Forever-but the words went like this:

"Do yer balls hang high? Do yer balls hang low?
Can you tie 'em in a knot? Can you tie 'em in a bow?
Can you throw them over yer shoulder like a European soldier?
Do yer balls hang low?"

No, I didn't sing it aloud but I kept step to the tune.

Old Blue Balls insisted that we go with him to Sulu's house before going to our own. "Oh, oh!" we thought, "Then he'll wallop us." But he didn't. All he said was to come to his office first thing next morning. I found it hard to sleep well that night.

I got it first and it was the strap, not The Hand. Mr. Donegal was all business and not smiling. "Bend over, Cully, and put your hands on the floor!" he commanded. I did. "Now repeat what I say after me!"

I had made a vow not to cry but when he said "I'll" and I said "I'll," POW went the strap. I couldn't help yelping. It was a hard lick right across my tail and it almost pushed me on my face.

"Never" was his next word. "Never," I whimpered. POW! Oh that strap hurt! I could feel it in my teeth.

"Play" came next, then "Hooky, and finally "Again" with that terrible strap burning my tail harder with every stroke. Despite my resolve I was crying when I left Old Blue Ball's office and it took me some time in the bathroom before I could bring myself to open the classroom door. Miss Polson smiled faintly as I let myself down into my seat and I could hear the other kids whispering "Cully got a licking. Cully got a licking." I learned later that Mullu and Fisheye each got one too but that Sulu didn't even get the ruler. All Blue Balls, I mean

Brown Balls, did when Sulu came into his office was to ask him if he was all right. Said he figured he'd had punishment enough but not to be truant again.

Oddly enough, I didn't get spanked by Dad that time though he said that Mr. Donegal had told him all about it.

Looking back, I think old Blue Balls enjoyed playing hooky too.

THE WISE MAN

Ben Tremblay made the decision to become a wise man shortly after he'd impulsively dived off the high granite cliff on the south shore of Lake Tioga. Almost breaking his back after that thirty foot drop, as he floated there on the surface barely being able to move his arms and legs, he realized that he was growing old. Yes, he was fifty years old with damned little to show for it. Oh, he had a tidy nest egg in the bank in Ishpeming, two guns, and a tight little cabin but no wife or family. No, he hadn't accomplished very much. If he'd had the education, he would have done more, maybe even done great things, for he'd shown early promise. Made 100's in every subject he took, including Latin, during his two high school years before he had to quit. He'd liked Latin. Oh, he'd read a lot of books since then and had educated himself but a jack of the woods needed only a strong back, not a brain.

All these thoughts came to him as he lay there aching in the water. How many more years did he have left to make something of himself if that were possible? He felt unfinished and perhaps that was a sign that he could do it. But what?

Suddenly, like a thunderclap, came the answer: He'd become wise! God knows, Tioga and the whole world needed wise men. If he really worked at it, maybe he could become one. It was a clear glorious vision so full of promise he immediately started becoming wise by swimming to shore.

Ben Tremblay knew that the task wouldn't be easy so he decided to take the next ten years of his life and devote them to the project. He got out his Bible and thought as deeply as he could about every single one of the proverbs. It was written there that "The hoary head is a crown of glory" so Ben began to raise a beard. If he were to become a wise man, he'd better look like one. There were grey threads in it when the whiskers appeared but eventually they'd be white enough. He had plenty of time.

The first real bit of wisdom that came to Ben was that he should start saying no. As he reviewed his past follies and frustrations, it was readily apparent that most of them had arisen because he hadn't said that word. *Yes* was the word of fools. Oh there were many times that it was hard to refuse a challenge or an invitation, as when his old friend Charlie wanted him to play another game of horse-shoes or to spend an evening at Higley's drinking, but over the long run Ben could see that his no's were simplifying his life and keeping him out of trouble. It was harder to say no to himself however, but by remembering that impulsive dive off the cliff, he often managed to do so.

The second bit of wisdom that came to Ben was that he must look at everything with strange eyes, as though he'd suddenly come to life in a world he'd never seen before. The practice of this insight gave him much pleasure. To see the infinitely varied blades of grass rather than just grass itself excited him. For the first time in his life he found a four leafed clover. Ben felt the bark of trees; he tried to whistle bird songs he'd never heard before or to put words to them. The white throated sparrow sang "Fiddle-dee, fiddle-dee, fiddle-dee." The twisted black moon-shadows of tree limbs on the snow almost made him ache with their beauty. The blue glint of the edge of his axe when sharpening it was a color he'd never seen before. At night in bed he felt the strong beating of his heart so vividly it was difficult to go to sleep. It kept saying "All's well! All's well!"

With this expanded consciousness, there also came a curious feeling of identification with the things he was observing. Once he became a berry bush with its tangled branches heavy with red fruit clusters. The long howl of the wolf in the grove made Ben's head lift. He found himself covertly assuming the postures and gestures of the people he met and, when he did so, it almost seemed as though he could know what they were thinking or feeling. Sometimes that was almost scary, but always it was exciting.

The next bit of wisdom that came to Ben Tremblay, as his beard grew greyer, was that he had to find some way of hanging on to the better thoughts that came to him. Many of them flew by so swiftly he could hardly see their nature. Almost like blue-winged teal, you had to look hard and fast to identify them. Also it was difficult to remember them. Somehow he discovered that they wouldn't disappear if he put his insights into words as soon as possible and so he started talking to himself aloud. For example, the thought vaguely came to him that he and others were too concerned about time. "Of course time was important," he said to himself aloud, "Even roses withered by the clock. No, not by the clock. The withering was of their nature and mine too. We all bloom and fade but need we measure loveliness by minutes? Ben stroked his beard, and then it came to him: "If you want a clock that always keeps time, just listen to your stomach." He said it aloud twice and wrote it down in a notebook.

As you can imagine, the whole town was puzzled by the change in Ben Tremblay. It was not just the beard; his whole face was different, sort of serene-like. "Maybe he's getting religion," someone suggested but that couldn't have been true. Ben never went to church. They noted how much time he spent alone on weekends when he came out of the woods from his lumbering job. "Yah, that's what happens to a man who never gets married," one woman said. "They get queer in the head." Oh, he was pleasant enough when you occasionally met him. He'd talk to you easily and friendly but he sort of seemed detached and far away at times, even when he was answering your questions. Up at the lumber camp, the only time he talked very much was when he was alone. People worried about that. Men who talked aloud to themselves might be going slow-crazy.

Also some of the things he'd say when talking to you were very strange even if they made a lot of sense. Like when he saw Mrs. Olafson giving her daughter a hard swatting for something bad she had done. "The child that is beaten, beats her doll" was what he said. That saying of Ben Tremblay's ran all over town. Again, when someone told him old Mr. Svenson had been caught trying to lift up a young girl's skirt, all Ben said was "Old mice like to look at new lard." When Don Jackson, an old friend of Ben's, suddenly died of a heart attack, he went to the funeral and told the bereaved wife, "Lightning always hits the tallest tree." A lot of the things Ben said were like that - strange, true, but a bit unsettling. Also, he didn't say them casually or off hand. They were pronouncements and we began to treasure them.

By the end of the ten years Ben Tremblay's beard was white and so were his eyebrows. Three notebooks full of hard earned wisdom sat upon the cabin shelf yet it seemed that the more he got, the less he had. Others were now calling him the Wise One. Indeed, when I was a kid, I thought his name was spelled Wisewon. People began to come to his cabin to ask for advice. Two of these were the Arfelin brothers, each of whom claimed he had shot the deer. Each insisted he had heard but one shot and there was only one big hole in the buck. After they had made their presentation and their arguments, the Wise One spoke. "Mene, Mene, Tekel, Upfarsin!" he said. "Split the deer down the backbone and each give the other first choice. Mene, Mene, Tekel, Upfarsin!" Then the word got around and someone asked Father Hassel what it meant, he said to look it up in the bible, in the book of Daniel.

When Mrs. Yntema came to the Wise One asking why her old hens were picking the new pullets to death, he frowned but gave her an answer. "At night in the dark all women and chickens are the same." That was all. Mrs. Yntema, after puzzling the words for some time took them to mean that she should take the pullets out of the chicken yard and put them back after midnight. The strategy was completely successful. So the Wise One's fame grew and grew.

Some of the problems people brought to him were very personal ones. One woman complained that she wasn't having any pleasure out of sex either because her husband was too quick on the trigger, or tht she was too slow. "If you want a hotter fire," he said, "use more kindling."

Referring to an arrogant but stupid man, the Wise One said, "The good Lord forgot to put any meat and potatoes in his pasty."

Speaking of unreasonable fears, he said, "You don't have to run till the skunk lifts its tail!"

Of unreasonable pride, he said, "The bigger the bubble, the sooner it pops."

Of hate and resentment, he counseled, "The wise man does not swallow a porcupine.

Some of the Wise One's sayings were a bit comical, and, as they were repeated all over town, we forgot the context in which they were spoken. Here are a few of them. "The thin louse bites the hardest." "Where the carcass is, there you will find the ravens." "It takes a big flea to lift a blanket." "The best laid eggs of mice and hens aren't always what they're cracked up to be."

When a young girl came to the Wise One to ask how she could keep from being pregnant, his prescription was "Only a still needle lets the thread enter."

When a mother, grieving for her dead child, came for understanding, he said, "It is as though the yolk were out of the egg."

To a sinner after he confessed the evil he had done: "Hell has no tomorrow!"

Of a lazy man: "There was no yeast in the dough when he was raised."

Of envy: "Every chub wants to be a trout."

Of foolhardiness: "If you don't enter the bear's den you won't get bit."

To a man complaining of his burdens: "The other man's packsack always seems lighter."

About an ungrateful son: "A man who forgets his father is a tree without a root."

Some of the Wise One's sayings still reverberate in Tioga today:
"The hottest sauna cannot clean a dirty heart."
"A rabbit has no choice when it's in the jaws of a wolf."
"Talk doesn't cook the potatoes."
"Better to have a net than just the desire to fish."
"More of a man goes down the outhouse hole than outside it."

"Dig the well before you're thirsty!"

"A poor man's dog is happier than a rich man's son."

"The bigger the hill, the more the horse farts."

"The more you pick at a wart the faster it grows."

When a pregnant woman asked the Wise One whether it would be a boy or a girl, he said, "The sun will set and the moon will rise."

When a Finlander asked him who would win the schoolboard election, this was his response: "Mene taalte hiiten." That means "Get the hell out of here!"

By the time he reached seventy, Ben Tremblay became very doubtful of his wisdom in becoming wise. So many people kept coming to him for counsel that he had hardly any time to meditate or enjoy. Indeed they came from miles around, from Michigamme, Republic and even Marquette to pester him with their troubles and questions. Often he found himself irritated rather than at peace. The fourth notebook had few entries. It was harder to sleep because he knew that when he spoke there'd be some fool at his doorstep asking another fool question. He had no time to cultivate his garden because of the interruptions. When once he escaped to go trout fishing so he could be alone, he noticed the reflection of his face in a quiet pool. The brow was furrowed and the face was not serene. Yes, it had been foolish to become wise. How could he free himself from the burden? How could he remove the curse of being known as the Wise One?

It took Ben Tremblay many weeks before he found the answer, and he rejected its enormity many times before accepting it. Somehow he would have to commit the ultimate folly, to do something so outrageously stupid, no one would ever call him Wise One again.

So Ben Tremblay bought himself a pair of glasses, the insides of which he painted black, and a cake of the beeswax we used to make our skis slippery, and he molded that beeswax into ear plugs that made it so he couldn't hear.

Then he married Aunt Lizzie, the yakkiest, nastiest, ugliest old woman in town.

OLD LUNKER

 limber Jim Vester was our town's champion liar. We had plenty of other liars but there wasn't a one who could come close to old Slimber. Some of his whoppers had been told and retold for years throughout our forest village. For instance, there was the one where he told about crossing a duck and a blue heron, the one about his old horse that could point partridge, the bullfrog that couldn't jump, how he caught Old Mustamaya, the great brook trout, using a posthole digger, and his famous bear story. Oh, there were a lot of them. Made us kind of proud to have the best liar in the U.P.

Slimber was kind of proud of his reputation but his real wish was to be known as the village's champion fisherman too. His catching Mustamaya meant something, of course, but Slimber had a rival in Louie Fachon, a little French Canadian who lived behind the depot and fished almost every day of his life. Unlike most of our people, Louie despised trout fishing. Too small, he said. "Me, I lak ze beeg poisson (fish) and me, I catch heem, oui!" Sometimes when he knew

Slimber would be down at Higley's saloon admiring his big stuffed trout behind the bar, he'd bring in a huge walleye or three foot long northern pike. "Now there, mon ami, is a feesh!" he would say to Slimber. "A sardine lak zat trout of yours, non! My feesh eat Mustamaya for bait. Why for you no try for ze beeg ones, eh? You don't know how, I sink (think)."

After several years of such needling by Louie, Slimber decided to start lake fishing. He'd catch a northern pike so big that Louie would have to shut up, maybe even big enough so Higley would have it mounted and hang it above his Mustamaya there in the saloon. Trouble was he didn't have a boat so Slimber tried fishing off the rocky points but without much luck. Finally for ten dollars he bought an old relic of a canoe from Untu Heikkala who had got it in trade for a hen and chickens. Untu had gotten it from Pierre de Sang who had found it on the shore of Log Lake where some sports from Chicago had discarded it because it leaked so badly. Slimber spent most of the winter repairing the canoe and making some paddles.

Lake Tioga is a big lake, ten miles long and one mile wide, large enough so winds can kick up some fairly hefty waves when the wind is from the west as it usually is. So Slimber, who'd never been in a canoe before, had to take about a month learning to handle the craft and fish at the same time. Mainly he trolled, using a red and white feathered spoon, with part of the line in his teeth and the rest in carefully laid loops on the floorboards. (He almost lost those teeth a couple of times when a good sized pike grabbed the lure). Also, the loops would get tangled, so Slimber built a little contraption out of a big wooden spool and piece of screen door spring that worked pretty good most of the time after he fastened it to a thwart. It allowed the hook to be set in the pike's hard bony mouth and yet would let out line grudgingly if the pull were hard enough. Slimber still had to haul the line in hand over hand however.

He found there was a lot to learn. For one thing, you had to be pretty careful when a big pike came near the boat. One of them tipped Slimber over into the drink when he failed to let go the line as the pike dove under the canoe. Then again, even if he had one in the canoe, the fish would thrash around something fierce, sometimes even jumping out of the boat again. Slimber learned to carry a hammer with him to tunk the fish hard between the eyes the moment it landed on the bottom of the canoe. Lifting a big one over the side is also a ticklish business especially if you don't have a net and Slimber didn't.

I should say something about the northern pike in Lake Tioga. They're a different breed. In the early 1890's Henry Thompson, our mining superintendent at the time, had a lot of Wisconsin fingerling northerns and muskellonge sent up in the water tender tank of a freight locomotive. They were dumped into Lake Tioga at the northeast end where the railroad skirts the shore. The little predators found our lake teeming with chubs, shiners, perch and some trout so they thrived. They also interbred resulting in progeny that were hybrids. Certainly, they had hybrid vigor. They grew larger, lived longer, and fought like hell when you hooked them. In later years, bass, walleyes and sauger were also planted so our tiger northerns, as we called them, had plenty to eat. Some of them grew to enormous size. I remember the two that my father and Grampa Gage had caught one evening. Displayed in our bathtub for the admiration of all, both fish were so long they curled up at both ends.

Another reason our tiger northerns were so big was that only a few of our men fished for them. In fact, besides Slimber's canoe, there were only three other boats hidden in the bushes at our end of the lake. Old man Elves used one of them every morning as long as he lived, fishing from dawn until nine A.M. when the passenger train blew its whistle at the railroad bridge. Titu Omalaina was out on the lake two or three times each week in his rowboat and the other regular was Louie Fachon who preferred evening fishing. None of them made a dent in the pike population.

I guess the reason most of us didn't fish for pike was that we couldn't bear sitting cramped in a boat for hours when we might be wading down a beautiful stream, hooking a speckled beauty of a trout at each bend or rapids. Besides trout were better to eat and easier to clean. Instead of having to scale or skin a northern, all it took with trout was one quick slit above the gills and another down the belly, then with a flip all the insides came out in one motion. Moreover, trout had none of those miserable forked pike bones that stuck in your throat no matter how carefully you tried to avoid them. Slimber felt the same way. He never cooked any of the pike he now was catching fairly regularly. Sometimes he'd bring a few home to use as garden fertilizer or to give to a Finn neighbor but usually he just threw them back into the lake.

No, Slimber Jim wasn't fishing for pike. He was fishing for glory and a chance to shut that fat mouth of Louie Fachon's forever. Over and over again he told himself that once he caught a really huge pike, maybe even Old Lunker himself, he'd never touch a damned paddle again. It was the thought of seeing that monster pike hanging over Mustamaya in Higley's saloon that kept him going back to the lake evening after evening.

I suppose every lake has its Old Lunker, the fabulous fish that always gets away. Several of our men had seen him or had him on the line. Six or seven feet long, they said, and weighing maybe sixty, seventy pounds, the fish grew bigger with each telling. One man claimed to have seen him swimming just under the surface, picking up seven ducklings, one after another and then swirling up to grab their mother with a mighty splash. Another claimed that he'd had

Old Lunker on his trolling line for two hours and had been towed by the fish half way to the end of the lake before the line broke. Said it was as long as an oar. Oh, there were a lot of tales like that. Slimber said he'd never tell such lies, that when he caught Old Lunker he'd bring it down and lay it right out on Higley's bar.

Trouble was, most of the pike he caught weren't big at all, most being only from four to six pounds in weight. His biggest was a ten pounder and when he showed it proudly to Louie, who usually came off the lake the same time he did, the dirty little French frog held up a stringer that held three fish much bigger.

This happened so often that Slimber knew he had to find out how Louie was catching the big ones. The Frenchman didn't seem to be trolling very fast, if at all, but when Slimber paddled over to see his lures, Louie rowed away. Finally, Slimber didn't fish at all one evening but instead walked the woods along the north shore of the lake making sure Louie couldn't see him. Peering through the bushes he saw that the Frenchman was still-fishing, using big chubs for bait. He didn't have a pole of any kind but he'd whirl his line to which a huge bobber and a shorter line were attached around his head several times, then let if fly out into the water. While Slimber watched, the bobber jiggled then disappeared, and after quite a battle Louie hauled in a big pike. "So that's how the bugger does it," thought Slimber. "Now I'll clean his clock!"

Slimber hated the new way of fishing. For one thing it meant having to get a new pail of chubs every time he went out, and keeping them lively enough to be worth anything; for another, it meant having to sit still in the canoe watching that silly bobber until he almost got hypnotized. At least when he was trolling there was something to do. The only thing that kept him at it was that he now was catching larger pike. Indeed, one evening when he and Louie came off the lake, he had a larger one than the Frenchman did.

Slimber also found that this new way of fishing required considerable skill and know-how. How deep should he set the bobber that he'd whittled out of white cedar? Well, it varied. On bright days, you set it higher on the line, further from the hook. How big a hook should he use? The bigger the fish, the bigger the hook. How could he keep a big pike from biting off the line? By using a short leader of picture wire or better yet an old mandolin string. How big a chub to use for bait? The bigger, the better - if he wanted the big ones. Slimber never really mastered Louie's technique of whirling the bobber and bait around his head and then slinging out the line. When he tried, time after time the chub flew off and he had to rebait. Finally Slimber just dropped the line and bobber overboard and quietly paddled away, then sat there in the canoe until something bit. Often it seemed to take a long time. It was hard to be so patient.

It was only by chance that Slimber finally located Old Lunker.

He'd been trolling across the lake and then up along the hardwood shore when suddenly something hit hard, yanking his spool contraption right off the thwart, over the gunwale and away. He watched it being pulled out into the lake. Occasionally the spool would surface, then disappear again. Slimber tried frantically to follow it but soon it was out of sight. He'd lost all his tackle but now at least he knew where an old lunker of a pike hung out.

The next morning with new line, bobber and hook, he went back to the same place. A sandbar had built up along the sides of a dead fallen spruce that extended outward from the shore into deep water where a little creek entered the lake. Slimber maneuvered the canoe as quietly as possible over the same spot, lowered the biggest chub he had into the water, and let the canoe drift almost to shore. Suddenly the float disappeared and the loops of the line in his lap uncoiled. Having previously lost a lot of pike by striking too fast, Slimber let the line slide between his fingers until it stopped. Then he jerked hard and knew he was onto a big fish. Heavy it was and strong! It took the line away despite all the strength he could muster, cutting his palms as it did so. A monster. Maybe Old Lunker! Slimber could see it hanging in the saloon.

But it was not to be. Suddenly the line went limp. Trying to arrange the line in his lap had given the pike its necessary slack to get away and Slimber pulled in only a very mangled minnow. For a week he fished the same spot without a strike and was about to hunt for another place when he saw a two pound bass or something leaping several times out of the water in a straight line. And something after it that looked like a dark slim alligator! Suddenly there was a big splash where the bass had been, then nothing more. Slimber was sure excited. That must have been Old Lunker, for sure. He decided that if Old Lunker had been after a bass that big, he needed bigger bait than the six inch chubs he'd been using.

Slimber spent most of the next day trying to catch suckers, big ones, in the pool under the Rolling Mill Dam. Always there had been red horse suckers in that hole but the day was bright and he only hooked one. At that he was thankful, carrying it back in the big bucket. Had he caught more, his arms would have fallen off on the four mile hike back to town. The sucker seemed kind of logy when he put it in the big perforated lard can in the creek that flowed out of the old mine pit but when that evening he put it in the bucket to go fishing it seemed active enough. Every so often as he paddled his way across to his lucky spot of spots, Slimber splashed in a new can of fresh water to keep the sucker lively.

When he got there he debated for a time about where to hook the sucker. He could hook it through the lips, or under the top back fin, or above the lower back fin. With the biggest hook he could find in his folder, he chose the last. He'd whittled out a larger bobber but even then the big sucker took it way down as soon as he put it in the water. Slimber paddled to the sand bar to sit and wait. At last the bobber reappeared and moved up and down a bit as the sucker swam beneath it.

Then all of a sudden down it went! Slimber watched it as it disappeared moving swiftly out into the lake. Again he laid out the line in his lap, loop by loop. "Lord, he's taken most of it," Slimber thought. "I've got to strike pretty soon or he'll have it all. But finally it stopped. "Let the bugger swallow it!" Slimber said aloud. "Wait, wait, wait!" Finally holding the line in both hands, he jerked as hard as he could. "I got 'im! I got 'im," he yelled.

I can't recall all the details of the epic struggle as told by Slimber though I've heard it several times. The loops of line in his lap tangled and he almost lost the fish. His hands became bloodied from line cuts when Old Lunker rushed for deep water time after time. When he hauled in line, the canoe went to the monster, not the fish to the canoe. Once the line wrapped itself around Slimber's thumb and almost cut it off. Another time Old Lunker almost hung it up on that dead-head log by the lily pads. Gradually the huge fish tired enough to let Slimber get him alongside the canoe. Then what to do? "I knew I couldn't get him over the side or he'd tip me over," Slimber said, "and if I stood up in that tippy canoe he'd kick around and dump me for sure. Lordy, oh lordy, what to do?"

In the end, Slimber just let out a bit of line and towed Old Lunker all the way across the lake to a sandy beach where, jumping out into the water, he dragged the monster almost to the bushes. Utterly exhausted, Slimber sat down on the sand until his heart slowed down and he could breathe again. He still could hardly talk when Louie Fachon beached his rowboat and came over to see.

"Sacre Bleu!" he exclaimed when he saw the fish. "Mon Dieu, such a poisson I nevair see before!" Louie spread his fingers and measured it hand after hand. "I sink zat feesh, she go forty-five, feefty eenches." he said enviously. "Forty pound peut-etre, maybe mor' " Oh how Slimber relished the moment.

As the two men started up the long footpath to town Slimber at first tried to hold the fish up in the air so it wouldn't get dirty but that lasted only about ten steps. The bugger was just too heavy and his hands hurt. So he broke and whittled a double forked hazelnut branch, put one of the forks through the fish's big gills, and began dragging it behind him. He'd clean it up later so it would look good there on Higley's bar.

That trail from the lake is a long one as all of us kids well knew. Not so bad going down Company Field hill to the lake for a swim, but coming back was always tough going. The path wandered first through heavy timber, then across the beaver dam and its surrounding muskeg, then through a thick spruce swamp until coming to the opening of the steep field. Slimber was pretty well bushed by the time he came to the clearing so he and Louie sat for a moment on a log to rest. Slimber was a bit tempted to needle his companion by giving unwelcome advice on how to catch the big ones but thought better of it. He might need Louie's help in dragging Old Lunker up that consarned hill.

Louie didn't offer either, not even when he saw that Slimber was getting exhausted when they were half way up. Instead he suddenly stopped and pointed down the path they'd been traversing. "Ze bear, she follow. Adieu, mon ami!" he cried, and high-tailed it for the grove at the top of the hill. Slimber took a look. Damned if there wasn't a big bear following them, snuffling the fish scent in the path.

Slimber wasn't really too concerned though because he'd bluffed too many bears in his time. If they came too close, all you had to do was start toward them. wave your arms and yell and they'd run away. Bears were scared of humans. Only when it was a big sow bear with cubs did you have to do any worrying. Besides, he didn't have far to go, just the rest of the way up the field and through the grove. But Slimber lengthened his strides just in case.

Now this happened in the year of the big June freeze, when it snowed hard on the twenty-third of the month and everything froze dead, fruits, potatoes and all. There were no sugar plums, pin cherries, blackberries or blueberries, not a one, and the bears were starving. Usually they only came out of the woods at night late in August to raid our apple trees but this year some of them had been turning over our garbage piles even during the day. One bear had broken into Mrs. Olette's summer kitchen and carried off a ham she was soaking. Although the bear meat was tough and useless, several bears had been shot in town when they became too much of a nuisance. They just didn't seem to have much fear of man that summer. Slimber knew these facts, of course, but tried to put them out of his head as he hurried faster. The big bear was gaining on him.

Bears are notoriously near sighted and this one, with his nose to the ground sniffing the strong fish smell, probably didn't even notice Slimber until, when they were only about thirty feet apart, the man made his move. Slimber dropped Old Lunker, charged toward the bear waving his arms and yelling like hell.

The bear stopped dead in its tracks, then rose up on its haunches and growled. "He looked ten feet tall," Slimber said later. "I waved and yelled again but that damned bear wasn't going to be bluffed. He wasn't after me but he sure was after that fish. That bear come closer, growling, and made a pass for it with his claws but I pulled it away. And then he just took a swipe, knocked it out of my hands, and run down the hill with Old Lunker in his jaws. Nothing I could do. Just sat down there in the grass and damn near bawled."

Badly in need of a drink, Slimber walked down to the saloon, and, after a couple stiff shots of Higley's rotgut, began to tell his tale. Always a fine story teller, soon a large group of men were hanging on every word. Slimber recounted the whole experience in minute detail, pausing every so often to light his corncob pipe and build up the suspense. When he came to the part about towing Old Lunker across the lake to the beach and laying it out there for Louie Fachon to admire, some man yelled, "But where's the pike, Slimber? Where's the fish?"

"I'm a-coming to that," said Slimber but when he told how he had fought the bear for the fish and lost, all the crowd started hooting in disbelief, slapping their thighs and laughing. Just another one of old Slimber's big lies!

"You don't believe me, hey?" Slimber had noticed that Louie Fachon was at the end of the bar. "Well, just ask Louie. He was there. He measured Old Lunker and helped me drag it up the hill till he saw the bear coming."

"Non," said the little Frenchman. "I see no feesh and I see no bear."

151

BITS AND PIECES

A mong my memories of Tioga as it was in the early years of this century are many little things that have no stories in them but yield glimpses of our people and the kind of a life we led. Let me try to capture them again.

When visitors came to Tioga from Down Below and wanted to see the sights, if any, we usually took them first to the cave in, a gigantic deep hole in the ground near the old mine. People said the ground had caved in because the miners had removed too much of the ore from the pillars that supported the surface earth and rock.

It happened one afternoon when I was playing in my sandpile. Suddenly the earth shook, then with a great roar a huge blast of dust obscured the sun. I ran into the house to cling to my terrified mother because I knew that there were deep caverns under my home too. Grabbing my younger brother and sister, mother and I ran down our hill street. Many other people were also running to the safety of ground that had not been undermined, but after that first terrible shock, nothing else happened.

Later we went up to the mine to see the damage. Along our street the cement sidewalks were cracked; some houses were askew on their foundations; the big windows of Flinn's store were broken and everywhere there was ore dust. Two houses had fallen into the great pit, one of them containing a miner who'd been sleeping because he worked the night shift. The great wheels atop the mineshafts were still and the people milling around talked in whispers to each other if they talked at all. A couple of days later some mine officials came down from Duluth and gave orders to close the mine immediately. Catastrophe!

I suppose it was hard for visitors to appreciate the significance of that cave in. All they could see was a five acre hole in the ground filled with dirty water. They couldn't understand that hundreds of lives had also caved in and that Tioga as a village almost died that afternoon too. No mine. No town. Yet Tioga survived.

We also showed our visitors the charcoal kilns and the ruins of the old stone furnace, three stories high, next to a forty foot waterfall. In the old days they smelted pig iron in the furnace using the charcoal from the bee-hive shaped kilns, then hauled the iron ingots to Marquette by wagons pulled by oxen.

Of course, we always took our visitors down to Lake Tioga with its many pine covered islands, rocky shores and sandy beaches. Perhaps we pointed out the wreckage of the old steam tugboat that once had hauled rafts of logs to the sawmill, or to the mine which, before the railroads came bringing coal, had only wood burning steam boilers for power. Coming back from the lake we called our visitor's attention to the old stage coach road that had been built from Menominee, Wisconsin, to Fort Wilkins at the end of the Keewenaw Peninsula in Lake Superior. Tioga had once been only a stage coach stop with a few cabins and barns where the horses could be changed.

Not much to see, really, so we always made sure our visitors saw Sieur LaFont's front door. LaFont was one of our favorite village characters and the stories of his laziness had circulated for years. The old man lived alone except for a big blue-tick hound named Bijou who was almost as indolent as his master. Well, one day LaFont got tired of always having to open the front door to let Bijou in and out so he cut a big hole in it so the dog could enter or exit whenever he wanted to. In the winter LaFont hung a flour sack over the hole on the inside of the door to keep some of the cold out and Bijou soon learned how to brush it aside. Then someone gave LaFont another dog, a fiesty little fox terrier, so LaFont sawed another smaller entrance hole for it. A big hole for the big hound, a small hole for the little terrier. When someone pointed out to LaFont that the small hole was unnecessary, the old man said, "That so? Why I nevair think of that?" but he winked outrageously.

No account of life in the U.P. would be complete without some talk about snow. Certainly the villagers talked a lot about it, sometimes with hate and sometimes with ruefull pride. The first snow came in October and the last could be seen in June some years. Once, on August the first, my father, Jim Johnson and I slept up at Dishno Lake in a snowstorm that lasted all night. It melted, of course, the next day.

We kids loved the snow more than our elders did. We made snow forts and igloos. In one monster drift that was twelve feet high Mullu and I spent a week excavating a cave that had three rooms. It was really warm in there after you'd been in it for a time and I felt pretty bad when my father broke open the roof with a shovel saying that it was too dangerous, that if it caved in we might smother.

Every winter we used snow to bank the foundations of our houses and barns. It really helped cut down the drafts on the floors. Also each winter my mother made a delicious custard, then put it out in a snowbank to freeze. Very good! Many of our people also boiled down their maple syrup from the year before then poured the thick liquid on clean snow to make maple wax, a candy we sure loved. For some of us it was the only candy we ever had.

Our snow was clean all winter long. At least it was after the mine closed down and the steel colored dust from its ore crusher no longer gave the snow a blue tint. As far as one could see, a frozen ocean of the purest white covered everything. Sometimes when one looked at one's ski or snowshoe tracks they almost seemed profane. I've tried in vain for years to find words that could capture a fir tree laden with heavy snow, one of the most beautiful sights in the world. An artist from Chicago once spent a year in a cabin four miles up the Tioga River, and occasionally I'd hike up there to visit him. People said he wasn't much of an artist because his paintings weren't' photographic but I liked them and the feelings they gave me. Most of them pictured our granite hills, or white water rapids, or they were snow scenes. I asked him once why he hadn't done one showing our fall colors. "No, They're too garish!" he replied.

He said he liked his snow pictures best. I guess I did too. There was one that showed ripples on the snow almost like those left by waves on a sandy beach, and another was full of snow contours so inviting you almost wanted to lie down and become a part of them. The paintings I recall most vividly though were of trees and tree branches casting shadows on new snow. Just black and white, they were, and the lines of those shadows almost seemed as though they'd been done by a Japanese. I still can't resist walking at night in the snow when there's a full moon to see those shadows.

They say that the Eskimos have seven words for the seven kinds of snow but no word for snow itself. Certainly it varies. The white fluff that lazily comes down early in the winter certainly differs from the sugar snow that can cut your face when the wind blows hard. Even when the great blanket of snow lay white on the ground your skis would know the different kinds when you went cross country.

But enough of snow! Lord knows, by March we'd all had our bellyfull of it and bitterly resented every new blizzard. Soon however the thaws came and little basins ringed every tree. Again we could see the tips of our picket fences. Huge icicles broke off from the eaves. With axes we broke off cakes of ice from our sidewalks and took down the storm doors and windows. Often we opened our windows and doors to let the spring air course through our houses.

As the snow water ran down the hill street all the kids in town built snow dams across it and screeched when a horse and wagon broke them down to let a flood of water loose. It was the break-up and no matter how wet and muddy we became, spring had come. No one can ever know the sheer delights of spring as vividly as we did in the Upper Peninsula of Michigan. Eric Niemi who lived all year long by himself in a shack by Horseshoe Lake with only a kangaroo mouse named Okkari for company claimed that the mouse and he danced three nights in a row when the snow was finally gone from the swamp.

I remember the first time I smoked. Mullu and I had wrapped some Indian tobacco in toilet paper to form cigarettes and asked Dick Deforrest for a match to light them. "Non, mes amis," the old Frenchman replied. "Zee weeds she is not good for smoke. You get seek." And then he filled his black old corncob pipe with Peerless, puffed it till it glowed and gave it to us. Mullu and I sure felt big puffing on that old pipe until the world revolved crazily and we heaved up our suppers. We were only seven. It took me many years before I began to smoke again and developed the dirty, filthy habit that I love. I never did smoke cigarettes but an old pipe is almost as much a comfort to an old man as an old woman.

There also was my first experience in a sauna. All the Finns in Tioga "went sauna" every Saturday night and occasionally at other times too. Back then we had communal saunas, big log, windowless buildings with many layers of benches surrounding the piles of stones heaped over the stove. Always there was a big barrel of water in the corner with a large dipper hung on its rim, and a box full of cedar branches with which to whip yourself after you'd taken all the steam you could handle. Although the Finn men and women segregated themselves in church, this did not occur in the sauna. Oh, there was some ogling, I suppose, but when you're trying to survive that wet heat, sex isn't very important.

My father was very opposed to the communal saunas, not out of any prudishness, but because he felt they were the prime reason why so many Finns developed tuberculosis. "You couldn't design a better environment for the spread of T.B.," he said. Nevertheless, I disobeyed him and, with Mullu and Sulu, had my first sauna there. They sure cooked me thoroughly, beat me with the cedar, then rolled me in the snowbank outside. Unlike smoking, I never tried a sauna again.

Memories of Tioga also bring back visions of the aurora borealis which we called the Northern Lights. Occasionally on a cool night we saw them as early as August month but the best ones came in winter. Great shafts of light shot up over the surrounding hills, shifting back and forth, almost as if in a cosmic, slow motion dance. Most of them were of a pale yellow or greenish color, but others were pink, almost reddish. We didn't know what caused the northern lights. One old Finn said that his grandfather had told him the gods were fighting one another over the horizon. No one could watch the northern lights very long without sensing their majesty.

There's more but that's enough. All I can say is that I'm sure glad I was born and grew up in the U.P.

If you have enjoyed the stories that Cully Gage has written in this THE LAST NORTHWOODS READER we know you will want to have and to read the first three volumes.

The first NORTHWOODS READER will introduce you to the lifestyles of the colorful characters who inhabited the Upper Peninsula in the early 1900's. The collection of eighteen stories will tickle your heart and soul and you will be anxious to journey through time with all these people.

In 1981 TALES OF THE OLD U.P. became the second Northwoods Reader and Cully again shares stories of his life and experiences in Tioga country. The rugged and loveable people about whom he writes were characters and victims of the time and even though you may never have known them you will relate to their humor and ingenuity. They're folks you will never forget reading about.

By the time you read HEADS AND TALES, the third Northwoods Reader, you will have acquainted yourself with the mischevious and entertaining antics of the generation who shared Cully's life and surroundings in their forest village. You may shed a tear or two in some of the reminiscing and we know you will chuckle aplenty at the humor of these stories. Of one thing we are sure---you will find it diffucult to close the book until you have read every one of the tales!

Cully says this fourth volume is THE LAST NORTHWOODS READER---we hope it will not be! It has been a great privilege to make these books available to our readers and the people of whom he writes will in this way live on for generations to come. Perhaps if you would write Cully Gage and ask him, as he did of his grandpa, for just one more he might reconsider.

Cully Gage's NORTHWOODS READERS are available from many bookstores and gift shops or may be ordered direct from Avery Color Studios, AuTrain, Michigan 49806.